I0731954

COVERT TACTICS

SEALS OF SHADOW FORCE: SPY DIVISION
SERIES, BOOK 5

MISTY EVANS

Copyright © 2023 by Misty Evans

Covert Tactics, SEALs of Shadow Force: Spy Division, Book 5

©2023 Misty Evans

Print ISBN: 978-1-948686-88-4

Cover Art by Fanderclai Design www.fanderclai.com

Formatting by Beach Path Publishing, LLC

All rights reserved.

No part of this book may be reproduced in any form or by any electronic or mechanical means, including information storage and retrieval systems, without written permission from the author, except for the use of brief quotations in a book review.

ONE

"This was a bad idea. Worst of the century, in fact," Rory murmured into his Bluetooth. The restaurant was packed, his cane barely finding a clear piece of real estate as he maneuvered past the various tables. Some patrons didn't notice him; the heavy curiosity or judgments of others felt like sticky spiderwebs on the back of his neck.

"You're fine, you big baby," Dr. Vivian Montgomery said in his ear. "Amelia will love this place, and you need to get out more. Win, win."

The latest addition to Shadow Force International was a royal pain in his ass. His boss, Beatrice Reese, who had employed the psychologist, and also insisted he take physical therapy from Dr. Amelia Thorpe, was an even bigger pain. The Queen B and Vivi had decided to play matchmakers. Like the two of them knew him better than he knew himself.

"I'm old enough to be her dad—and she's..." He wasn't

sure how to explain it. Explain *her*. Amelia, even at work, dressed in heels and designer suits. She carried six-hundred dollar handbags, and had her hair styled every week at some fancy salon. He never wore anything but camo pants and T-shirts, most with holes in them. He occasionally combed his hair, preferring to wear it in a low ponytail at the base of his neck, and his beard was months past a good trim. "She's so goddamn far above my class, she shouldn't even give me the time of day."

"Stop with the self-sabotage." He heard the squeak of Vivi's chair. She really needed to grease it. "We talked about this. The difference in your ages is not that much—she's thirty-one."

She looked far younger.

Following the host, he finally made it to the table he'd reserved for the two of them overlooking the D.C. lights. This was definitely Amelia's type of place. He was content at the local bar and grill, or staying in his room at SFI with a microwave dinner and a football game. "She deserves better. When she finds out the details about my background..." The guy frowned, but handed him a menu. Rory pointed to the Bluetooth in his ear, hiding his cane on the other side of his chair. "Sorry, my therapist never cuts me any slack."

The host had the good sense not to comment and gave a fake smile as he stuffed a second black bound booklet in front of Rory. "Our wine menu. Would you like to order a bottle so it can breathe before the other party gets here? I can recommend the Bordeaux 89. A unique vintage with stellar body. The Haut Brion Blanc, in fact, is considered one of the best white Bordeaux wines ever produced."

Hell, he knew nothing about snooty drinks, but Amelia would probably love it. "Give me a minute, would you?"

"Of course." The man half-bowed and hurried away.

"She's not here yet." Had probably changed her mind. That was better for both of them, wasn't it?

Vivi sighed. "Take a deep breath and relax. She is habitually late, you know that. If I had to guess, I bet she's as nervous as you are."

He ignored the menus and the lingering gazes of those who found him more interesting than their dinner. "Who could blame her? She's finally come to her senses and realized I'm a loser and I can never give her the kind of life she wants. *Deserves*."

"You sound like a man in love, and here I thought this was nothing more than a casual date. That's what you insisted it was when you were in my office last time, wasn't it?"

He dragged a hand across his face and stared at the night filled with city lights that seemed to mock him. This town had made him, and then broken him. His SEAL days were long past, his ghost work for the government a bit more recent. While Amelia knew some of his history, as did most of those who worked for Shadow Force, it was top-secret and there was a reason he stayed hidden in the bowels of SFI. She had no clue about the things he'd done for his country. Sure, some were heroic, but others tars less so.

In all honesty, he should've been six feet under with the terrorists and dictators he'd taken out. Would have been, if not for Beatrice and her husband, Cal Reese. Along with Emit Petit, who'd founded Shadow Force, the infamous Rory Tephra would have been nothing more than the legend he'd created for himself—a ghost.

"What do I do if she *does* show up?" It was a longshot and he knew it, but his knee wouldn't stop bobbing under the table, his gaze flicking to the entrance. Along with the rest of SFI, Amelia had given him a reason to live—and he was walking again, thanks to her and her therapy routine.

"You enjoy a night with a smart, beautiful woman." This was said with a *duh* tone.

He took out his phone and typed a text to Amelia. *Something's come up. Sorry, I can't make it.* His thumb hovered over a sad face emoji. She'd be relieved. Was probably at this moment trying to come up with an excuse to blow him off.

Yet, he couldn't bring himself to hit *Send*.

The soft murmur of voices and occasional laughter was normal for a high-priced, popular restaurant like this, but it grated on his nerves. It took everything in him not to jump up and run. Of course, *running* was technically out of the question, but he could move pretty quickly with his cane. "I'm a disabled freak. The only reason she said yes to this is because she feels sorry for me."

Another tight sigh issued from the other end of the call. "You're right. You should just go home." He heard the snap of Montgomery's briefcase, a sound with finality to it. "Spend the rest of your days as a hermit, getting your thrills from hacking into top secret government files and watching the rest of us have full, exciting lives. You don't deserve happiness, right? And you certainly don't deserve Amelia, who's helped you overcome the mental block that kept you in a wheelchair, and who lights up like a firecracker every time she sees you in PT. Every damn time, she sees you, period. Go ahead and break her heart, asshole. She'll be in my office next week crying over you. I can hardly wait."

The raw vehemence in her tone took him aback. "What...?" And then he caught on. "I know you're a genius, but I am no idiot. I see what you're trying to do here, Doctor, and I don't appreciate it."

"I don't appreciate you wasting my time. Order the wine, smile when she arrives, and remember the questions we scripted in your session last week. All you need to do is act human for a couple hours. Stretch goal—try charming. Forget about your age and past. This is about your future, Rory. You're allowed to have fun, and Amelia is nuts about you. Don't fuck this up."

He typically appreciated her directness, but tonight, like everything else, it annoyed him. Stretch goals—she was always making him go after shit way out of his comfort zone. Acting as if he were normal. As if he had charm in spades, rather than less than a teaspoonful. Hell, he didn't even have that much.

If he hadn't been sitting in the midst of dozens of people, he would've taken the Bluetooth from his ear and fired it across the room into the wall. Instead, he heard Vivi disconnect, effectively handing him the reins of his own life to control.

Which was exactly what she was supposed to do. *Damn it*. She'd outsmarted him again.

Brooding for a minute, he toyed with his options. He could shoot off that message to Amelia and cancel, letting her off the hook. He could sit here and be embarrassed when she canceled on him.

Or...he could wait and see if she showed up.

Stretch goal.

He glanced at the door, swallowed his pride, and loosened the tie around his neck. Picked lint from his jacket. Fiddled with his napkin.

When the waiter approached with two glasses of ice water, he tried to smile, found it was too much to ask, and attempted to not growl instead. "The maître d' mentioned an '89 Bordeaux." After the guy's description of it, Rory didn't want to know how much it cost. "I'd like to start with a bottle of that."

The waiter looked thrilled. "Marvelous choice. A unique vintage," he echoed. "You must know your wines. I'll be right back."

"Yeah, I know a lot about unique vintages." *Myself included.* "You don't happen to have Michelob on tap, do you?"

The waiter hesitated, his brows dipping. "A glass of that, too?"

Rory nodded and the guy scurried off.

The lights in the distance winked at him. He would try to be human, maybe even *charming.* He used to be able to turn it on and off without even thinking. *Used to.* Life was so different now. He snorted to himself. Being charming was definitely too much of a stretch.

But he had rehearsed those questions Montgomery had given him to ask Amelia—How to Make Polite Conversation 101—and maybe, if he was lucky, he would indeed not fuck this up.

TWO

Amelia Thorpe was running late.

Again.

Story of my life.

Vivi had told her being late was a sign that she really didn't want to do whatever she'd agreed to. That if she were truly invested in the person, situation, or occasion, that she would show up on time or even early.

Amelia had never been early in her life, even to things she genuinely wanted to participate in. She always wanted to believe it was a genetic fault—her mother had been the same—but she had to admit that Dr. Montgomery knew far more about the human psyche then she did.

Worrying her bottom lip, she stared at her phone. She'd left her appointment with her friend, Hannah, happy and excited for this time with Rory. While she'd been keeping their relationship—or whatever this was between them—a secret, she'd spilled the beans to the First Daughter during her rehab session on her wrist. She hadn't mentioned Rory's name, only that she was looking forward to dinner at this restaurant and hoping she never had to look at a dating app again.

The twenty-eight-year-old had squealed like a teenager with delight and demanded details. Normally, Amelia went to the White House for the sessions since Hannah's mother had recently had hip replacement surgery and was relying on her daughter for help. Hannah had unfortunately injured herself while moving her mother from the bed to a chair and the two of them had enlisted Amelia for therapy.

Hannah, always on the go and traveling the world, had confided she was glad to be there for her mother, but she was bored silly. Only the planning for her upcoming fundraiser had given her something to focus on. She was scoping out the event location and finalizing the details that day and, since she'd be less than ten blocks from SFI, had requested they do it there.

There weren't many places deemed safe enough for the president's daughter by the Secret Service, but SFI Headquarters was one of them.

That was due in part to Rory's vigilant security system. He was smart, calculating, and seemed to know exactly how criminals, terrorists, and war lords thought.

That wasn't *too* disturbing.

He was probably worried about her at this very moment. *I should let him know I'm running late.*

"Looks like we have a traffic jam," Jose, the proud owner of J-Dog Ride Service, said from the front seat of his older Mitsubishi. The car had probably been cute and sporty in its younger days, but now seemed old and smelled of fried food.

Amelia groaned at the flash of red taillights ahead. Of course there would be a traffic quagmire in D.C. on the one night she needed there not to be. When wasn't there? This snarl could take an hour to untangle, making her even later.

The ride service driver, a friend of Hannah's—ever since they were fifteen at volleyball camp, Hannah made friends everywhere she went—glanced at Amelia in the mirror. "I'd take a side road detour, but I can't even get to the next one. We're stuck."

Cars were bumper to bumper in both lanes on either side of them and the nearest escape was a block away. Amelia swore under her breath. "Karma is a bitch."

"Excuse me?" Jose asked.

"Nothing." She'd been rude to Hannah's lead Secret Service officer, Cohen Masden, when he'd demanded to search her upon Hannah's arrival and again when she'd left. Like, what kind of bull hockey was that? Hannah was her friend above all else, and she would never harm her or do anything like record their conversations. Amelia cared little about what went on behind closed doors inside the White House, except where Hannah's health and welfare were concerned. This was their third appointment and it riled Amelia that because it took place at SFI, Masden assumed he could be extra pushy.

While Hannah was an adult and didn't live with her parents normally, she was actively involved in politics and doing everything she could, while her dad was the leader of the Free World, to make it a better place. She'd started a foundation, gathering social media influencers around the world to create change in ways the younger generation aspired to. Leading Edge, or LEAD, as it was nicknamed, brought the children of world leaders together with those directing social media platforms and created international friendships. Together, they set up scholarships, internships, and grants for young entrepreneurs like Jose.

Amelia didn't actually believe in karma, but she wanted to, especially when a jerk like Masden insinuated she was willing to betray Hannah to get ahead in Washington.

"It's his job," Hannah had said, trying to smooth over Amelia's irritation. "Don't take it personally."

An hour later, Amelia was still trying to shake it off. "How far is it to the restaurant?"

Jose checked his GPS. "Three blocks if we could zigzag through a few back alleys."

So close and yet so far. Amelia eyed her three-inch Binni Nali heels and worried her lip again. Another up and coming influencer in the world that Hannah had introduced her to, the Korean designer was known for her mixed striped compositions and geometric patterns. Amelia loved all of her shoes and handbags.

Amelia enjoyed supporting small businesses and especially those LEAD promoted. Hannah had asked her to join the foundation's board, and she was considering it, but with the upcoming move from the current SFI Headquarters near downtown to the new site up north, her travel time back and forth to meetings would put a crimp in her work schedule. She had to be available at odd hours for the men and women who worked for Shadow Force and its cover company, Rock Star Security. There were no nine-to-five positions when it came to bodyguard assignments and paramilitary operations. Just like the other employees who worked round the clock in all types of scenarios and situations, Amelia needed to be flexible and available at a moment's notice. It wasn't the job for everyone, but she loved it.

"How much do I owe you?" she asked Jose.

"You're bailing on me?"

"It's a pleasant night and I can hoof it the rest of the way." She opened her tote, a match to her shoes, and took out her Betsey Johnson platform sneakers. While not as comfortable as her running shoes, they did catch the streetlights with their rows of rhinestones. "It's D.C.—I'm always prepared to walk."

As late as I am, I'd better run.

She paid Jose and thanked him, waving off his protests against taking the alley route he'd suggested. "It might be dangerous."

She exchanged the shoes on her feet, tucking the heels into the bag and patting it. She had a palm-sized stun gun, Rory approved, that she carried everywhere. "I'm prepared for that, too."

The kid frowned. "Are you sure?"

Grabbing the door handle, she slid out and smiled at him. "Have a great night!"

She took off at a fast clip, checking her app for directions. She'd lived here for several years but always got turned around. Maybe her lack of direction was genetic, as well.

Traffic jam, she typed in a text to Rory, dodging a few

people on the sidewalk. The first of two alleys she needed was ahead on her left. *On my way, but running late. Sorry.*

His reply was nearly instantaneous. *No problem. I'm just sitting here enjoying some wine.*

She chuckled, skirting a group of kids gathered at the corner and finding the path she needed. *Liar. You hate wine.*

He sent a winky face. *How did you know?*

She knew a lot, but nothing more important than insignificant things such as that. He loved basketball and axe throwing. Typically wore nothing but camo pants and t-shirts. Wouldn't eat rice or tofu and would devour a gallon bucket of pistachio flavored ice cream in one sitting. His favorite movies were action adventure (no surprise there) and he hated rom-coms.

He was built like a tank but his time in the wheelchair had caused his leg muscles to weaken. Together they were working on that and he was once again seeing them grow and gain strength. While he acted as if it was no big deal, she knew it was actually the biggest. Walking again, being able to feel normal, both excited and terrified him.

I have my ways. She jogged down the alley, past a dumpster. It was darker than she'd imagined and she had to hop over a few puddles of nondescript "stuff." The smell was atrocious and there was no way she was subjecting her pretty shoes to whatever lay in them. *You may have been a SEAL, but I'm a woman. I *know* things.*

He sent back a series of laughing emojis. *Noted.*

She couldn't keep the grin off her face, holding the phone to her chest for a moment. His texts were usually dry and lacking any hint of his personality. Even that was typically sarcastic and acerbic, especially with the other former SEALs. Tonight, he was almost...dare she say it?...*charming.*

So not him. Maybe getting him away from SFI was the trick. Ideas about what to type back to keep the conversation going filled her head. She turned right onto a lighted sidewalk and breathed a sigh of relief, but it was packed with gawkers, checking out an accident.

Traffic was still backed up and the sound of sirens flooded the night air. She squeezed between a few onlookers gathered in front of a closed deli and bumped her knee against a stone planter. "Ouch. Excuse me."

They didn't move and she shoved in front of them, using her bag as leverage.

It was like trying to move through molasses, and she continued yelling, "Excuse me! Coming through!"

The scene showed no one was seriously injured, and since she was already late, she left it to the police and medics to sort out. When she was at the curb, she checked her screen again, then the street signs. Turning right, she took off down that walkway, less crowded thankfully, and caught the scent of Italian food.

Two blocks down, the alley she needed came into view. She reread Rory's texts and sent a final message to him. *Almost there.*

She couldn't wait to see him, even though it had only been five hours since he'd been in the gym with her, doing leg presses. This was different. They weren't at work. They could flirt and not be under anybody's scrutiny. Maybe she'd coax a bit of info from him about his past. He always claimed it was confidential, and she wasn't one to press any of the SFI employees on sensitive subjects, yet she knew it would do him good to at least tell her about his accident. She was his physical therapist, after all.

And his friend.

Dare she hope she could be more?

For the first time in years, she was attracted to someone romantically. It made no sense—he was absolutely *not* her type in the least, but maybe her type was changing. Evolving. Expanding.

The blow came without warning and pain exploded in the back of her head. Her vision whited out, her ankle twisted painfully, and she fell face-first onto asphalt. *Smack.* Her forehead hit the wet ground and she gasped. The quiet but weighted smack of shoes echoed around her. A shadow fell over her. She blinked rapidly to get her eyes to clear.

Her head swam and somewhere in the recesses of her mind she was screaming, but no sound came from her lips. All she could do was whimper.

In her peripheral vision, she saw the shadow snatch up her tote. When she'd fallen, she'd sent it skittering across the ground, right through another puddle of unknown contents.

Footsteps. Striding.

At least they were moving away.

Her ankle screamed along with the voice in her head, hot, stabbing agony radiating up her calf, even as a similar agony filled her head and neck.

"Help," she managed to squeak.

The sirens had arrived and there was no one close enough to hear her over the noises of them nor the crowd.

Her pulse beat in her ears and her phone dug into her ribcage.

Phone! *Rory.*

Fighting the nausea and vertigo when she shifted onto her side, she moaned. Her fingers felt around, grazing the cell's case. Latching onto it like a lifeline, she eased it up to her face.

She dropped it twice before she gave up and left it on the ground, shifting her pounding head in order to read the screen. Everything was blurry and she sobbed trying to blink her vision into submission. With a trembling finger, she found Rory's avatar and hit his number.

He answered on the first ring. "Hey. Did you make it? I'm all the way in the back, near the windows."

"Ro...ry?" Spots danced at the edge of her vision. The alley had grown darker; all she could make out was the light from her phone. Exhaustion swamped her, her stomach somersaulting. *"Help...me."*

His response sounded too far away as the complete and utter darkness tugged her under.

THREE

Rory shot straight to his feet, nearly upending the table. The beer the waiter had brought tipped over, spilling onto the white tablecloth and clanking against the wine glass opposite him. "Amelia," he yelled into his phone.

When it had vibrated inside his jacket pocket, he'd assumed it was Montgomery calling to check on him, or perhaps Beatrice. He was on call twenty-four seven, and rarely left the compound. While he more than deserved a night off, being available to the paramilitary teams in the field was paramount.

His text conversation with Amelia had made him smile—rare these days. He'd been struck by the fact that she *got* him. She wasn't offended by his sarcasm and laughed at his jokes. Perhaps Vivi was right—was it possible? Amelia *liked* him. *Really* liked him.

But it hadn't been the SFI psychologist or the Queen

Bee calling him. His face split with a big smile when he saw Amelia's number, then he experienced a moment of panic. What if she'd changed her mind as he'd anticipated? What if she *wasn't* coming?

He...lp...me. Her voice—weak and tremulous—echoed in his ears.

Then silence.

He grabbed his cane, bumping the table again. The glass fell this time, breaking as it hit the fine China. The patrons around him were staring now has he hustled as quickly as he could to get past them to the exit.

"I'm coming," he said into his phone, fumbling between it and shoving a waiter out of the way. The poor guy stumbled into the back of a chair, losing his grip on the tray of food he carried. It ended up in a woman's lap and she screamed.

The maître d' was calling after him, telling him to stop, that he had to pay for the bottle of wine. Rory blasted past, his cane catching the guy's foot and tripping him.

He didn't stop to help him up. "Amelia! Talk to me!"

There was nothing but background noise on the connection. A waiter rushed forward and tried to stop Rory from going through the front doors. He shoved the kid aside, nearly knocking down a couple entering the restaurant.

The man cursed him, but Rory kept going out into the night. He wasn't up for driving yet, and had used a ride service, so he had no vehicle. He fumbled with his phone, going to the app that could track any of the SFI employees via their SIM card. With a shaking finger, he scrolled through the names until he found Amelia's and hit the tracking button.

While he waited, he turned in circles, wanting to move, *needing to get to her*, but not knowing which direction to go. She always used a car service as well to jet around the city. Had she been in an accident?

Come on, come on, come on. He shook the phone as if that would speed it up. Checked how many bars he had—they were full—and started hobbling down the sidewalk, because he couldn't stand still any longer.

The maître d' had recovered and rushed out the door, yelling at him about paying and the mess that he made inside. Demanding he come back.

Get to her. "Sorry! I'll pay later!" He kept hobble-running away from the building.

The app's GPS finally locked in, giving a soft *ding*. In that moment of sheer panic, it was the most beautiful sound he'd ever heard.

Amelia was close. His head swiveled to the left, seeing a narrow path between the restaurant and the building next-door. It wasn't big enough to even be an alley and the restaurant had placed a topiary there, hoping to keep people out.

It was the quickest way to get to where he needed to be. Rory pushed the large plant out of his way. The pot was so heavy, it simply tipped, sending dirt scattering over the sidewalk, and forcing Rory to climb over it.

His broad shoulders wouldn't fit easily between the brick walls, so he had to turn sideways to squeeze down the cramped path. As he did so, he sent out a Code Yellow

—the SFI version of SOS—to anyone in the area. The app told him the closest people were Parker Jeffries and Morris "Moe" Bouchard, otherwise known by his Rock Star code-name, Henley.

The other end of the path opened up, and Rory's insides dropped to his knees. He was in the alley behind the restaurant, and there was a figure on the ground.

"Amelia!" He hobbled as fast as he could to get to her. What was she doing here? Had the driver dropped her off in the alley?

Fucking idiot.

His cane slipped in a greasy spot and he fell, cursing as his knees hit the ground. He managed to accidentally boot the cane on the way down, and it spun out of reach, smacking into a wheel on the dumpster and disappearing under it. "*Fuck!*"

Hauling himself up, he barely registered a warm wetness running down one of his shins beneath his pants. The fabric had torn and the gritty asphalt had ripped open his skin.

He took a step, and his busted knee sent sharp pain up and down his leg. Without his cane he was off-balance and tumbled, banging into the dumpster and ricocheting off it.

His weak legs screwing him over, he ended up on all fours, unable to stay upright and balanced enough to walk. "Goddammit," he swore violently under his breath, and then he started crawling. "I'm coming, Amelia."

He repeated her name over and over again until he reached her side. "Shit. What happened? Talk to me."

She didn't so much as move and fear raced through

him. He slammed the door on it and ran his now dirty hands over her, searching for an injury. His fingers came up sticky and wet when he touched the back of her skull, and he yanked out his phone to use the flashlight to get a better look.

"Oh no. No, no, no." His guts turned to ice as the light illuminated her unconscious form. Taking in the amount of blood from the wound, he steeled himself to slip his fingers along her neck to find her artery.

Don't be dead. Don't be dead. Please, God, don't let her be dead.

He held his breath, his own pulse creating a racket in his ears, his heart beating too hard. Squeezing his eyes shut, continuing his plea to whatever higher power might exist, he nearly cried out with relief when he felt a slow, but thready beat under his fingertips.

Ever so gently, he brushed a strand of hair out of her face. He was afraid to move her in case there was damage to the vertebrae in her neck or back, but he could see no other wounds, outside the obvious one.

Even as he checked her breathing, and managed to dial 911, he kept going over the questions beating against his brain like a timpani. Why the hell was she in the alley? Who had done this?

He desperately wanted to move her, to pull her into his lap to cradle her, but he'd seen his fair share of injuries in the field. Hell, he had experienced enough of his own to know better. He was no doctor, although he'd patched himself up numerous times to keep from ending up in the hospital and blowing his cover, and the best thing he could do right now was to slow the bleeding and make sure she stayed warm.

The next moments passed far too slowly as he covered her with his jacket, ever so gently pressed his handkerchief against the wound, and held her hand until Parker and Moe arrived. A squad car and an ambulance did as well within seconds after them, and he explained to everyone what had transpired.

It was damned little to go on.

The cops gave him the third degree while Parker retrieved his cane from under the dumpster and handed it back to him. The EMTs worked on Amelia in the light from the squad car, and one said, "You should get that knee checked out."

He didn't so much as glance down, his focus on Amelia as the medics gently placed her on a gurney. He started to follow them to the ambulance when the cop who'd been taking notes said, "You the guy who skipped out on your tab?" The asshole pointed at the back of the restaurant. "Sounds like you did a lot of damage in there, as well. I'm going to have to write up a citation."

Moe typically annoyed the shit out of Rory, but tonight he was an angel in disguise. "I'll take care of it. Come on, officer." For whatever reason, he'd ditched his usual British accent and sounded a hundred-percent American. "The guy's lady was attacked. You can't tell me that under the same circumstances, you wouldn't bust through walls to get to someone you loved."

Parker jutted her chin towards the ambulance. "Go," she told Rory. "We'll handle this."

On trembling legs, he busted his ass to catch up with the EMTs.

THREE HOURS LATER, he sat in a hospital room listening to the beeping monitors and watching the rise and fall of Amelia's chest under a faded ivory blanket. She had yet to wake up, and the doctor on call had ordered a series of tests, including an MRI and CT scan of her brain.

So far, the only thing he'd been told was that she had a concussion and a hairline fracture in her ankle. The medical staff were obviously worried about brain damage, but nobody would come out and say it. He was so angry, so beside himself because he couldn't do anything to help her, he wanted to punch someone.

Beatrice had brought him his laptop and a fresh set of clothes. Dr. Montgomery had shown up with his largest travel mug filled with his favorite brand of coffee.

"Moe traced her movements prior to the alley," Beatrice told him. Moe was an average hacker, and better at things like interrogation. Tonight, however, he was proving to be more useful than Rory expected. "She completed a physical therapy appointment with Hannah Clemson, cleaned up at her apartment, then used a ride service to get to the restaurant. There was a fender bender a few blocks away, and Jose, the driver, claims she insisted on walking the rest of the way when they were caught in the resulting traffic jam. He tried to dissuade her but she insisted she'd be fine. Since her handbag is missing, the police are ruling it a mugging."

"Is it her Binni Nali?" Vivi asked.

Beatrice shrugged. "I hope not. That's her favorite."

"She has a duplicate, I think." Vivi said. "She does that sometimes—buys two so she can use one for daily wear and tear and keep the other for special occasions."

Like that mattered. Although... He ran a search of the designer's line of purses and there. *That one.* He'd seen her lugging it around headquarters. He'd check for anyone carrying the trendy, and downright ugly—in his opinion—bag.

Which might be half of D.C.

He'd refused medical treatment for his knee, and was running his programs, searching for cameras in the area that might have caught the attacker. He didn't bother looking up. "Any leads on the assailant?"

"None so far." Beatrice leaned against the window ledge next to Vivi. "What's your gut say?"

He glanced at the bed and Amelia's still form. If only she would wake up so he could question her. "None of her jewelry was taken. She still had her cell. Hell, even those ridiculous shoes she was wearing are worth a lot on the street. Why did the fucker only steal her purse? Why knock her unconscious in order to do so? She's not exactly hard to overpower. Easy enough to simply yank the thing from her shoulder and run. Maybe knock her to the ground in the process, but why clobber her in the back of the head?" Molten lava burned in his stomach. "Feels like overkill. Or something more personal."

"It *was* overkill. A vicious blow, almost as if the assailant was angry." Vivi walked to the side of the bed and stared at Amelia. She touched her hair. "But whoever it was might've gotten scared, especially if it was someone young—a kid. They saw an opportunity, knocked her in the head, took the bag and ran."

We're damn lucky she's still alive. "Or she fought back and that's why they hit her," he countered.

"There are no defensive wounds," Beatrice pointed out, joining Vivi at the bedside. "Knowing Amelia, she would've tried to talk to them, not fight them, but I can't help thinking if she resisted, they would have hit her face-on, not come from behind."

He agreed. The current traffic camera Rory had hacked into showed Amelia leaving the Mitsubishi and jetting down the sidewalk out of sight. He hadn't found one closer to the alley, but he would. "True enough. It still seems...off."

"Do you want me to keep Moe and Parker on this with you?" Beatrice asked.

Before he could respond, the on-duty nurse hustled through the door. Exasperated, she pinned each of them with a condemning scowl. "This is the Intensive Care Unit. As I told you previously, visitors are limited to one at a time, and"—she made a show of checking the watch on her wrist—"what do you know? Visiting hours were over *two hours ago.*"

"I'm not going anywhere." Rory stared at the screen in front of him, fingers flying over the keyboard.

"We'll see about that. I'll call security."

The squeak of her shoes grated on his nerves as she turned and marched to the door. The boiling lava wanted —needed—an escape valve. He started to yell at her to leave them the fuck alone, but Beatrice shot him a *stand down* glare and intercepted the nurse before she got to the exit. "You've been very lenient and I apologize for breaching the rules, but our coworker's family won't be here until tomorrow." She'd contacted Amelia's parents in South Carolina, and they were taking the first flight out in the morning. "We're all she's got at the moment, and one of us needs to be here when she wakes up. She's been through a terrible experience and may be scared to find herself in the hospital." She brushed the nurse's elbow with a hand and gently guided her toward the hall. "Perhaps we can discuss this further with Dr. Houston. He's already given us permission to keep somebody with her at all times due to the sensitive nature of her work."

The way Beatrice emphasized the last few words, something clicked for the nurse. She paused, scrutinizing first B and then the rest of them, ending with Amelia. Her voice lowered. "Is she a spy? We don't usually get them in here. Occasionally, we might get an important patient, or those whose identity is *covert*."

She sounded entirely too excited about that idea as Beatrice led her outside. The door closed with a quiet but firm click.

For a brief moment—too brief, in Rory's opinion—silence reigned. Only the steady beat of the heart monitor broke it, and the shadowy room enveloped him. Taking a deep breath, he almost relaxed, knowing he wouldn't be forced to leave Amelia's side.

"It's not your fault, you know."

He couldn't help it, he glanced up at the psychologist. *How does she always know what I'm thinking?* Stress and adrenaline once more churned through his system, and he wanted to tell her to go to hell, but dammit, she gave him *that* grin that told him she knew exactly how he was cursing her out mentally, and she wasn't scared of him and his damning glare. "I don't need you to analyze me. Go home."

"Sounds like you're giving me orders."

He sighed, continuing to search footage from security cameras. There were plenty that had picked up the crowd around the accident, but he couldn't pinpoint any closer to the alley, not even when he searched for someone carrying a purse like Amelia's. "As if you would take them."

"I need to drive this home, as your friend as well as your therapist—it's not your fault she was mugged."

"If I hadn't invited her to dinner..."

She strolled to the end of the bed, hands on hips. "You didn't cause her to run late. Nor did you cause the accident. Oh, and wait. You didn't suggest she leave her ride and walk alone in a dark alley. You are *not* to blame for everything that goes wrong in the world, Rory Tephra. Stop acting as if you are."

If only he could. He rubbed his face with a scarred hand. "I told you it was a bad idea and it was."

A soft, tremulous voice came from the bed, startling both of them. "What was a bad idea?" Amelia asked.

He jumped to his feet so quickly the laptop fell to the ground. His swollen knee gave out and he crashed into the side of the bed, barking in pain. Vivi reached out to try and help him, only he shrugged her off, using the railing to steady himself as he bent over Amelia and brushed the strands from her forehead. "Hey there."

"Rory? Where am I?"

"The hospital. You were mugged."

"Is that why my head hurts?" She raised a trembling hand to touch her neck, where a thick bandage protected the wound. "How is that your fault?"

He glanced at Vivi and she arched a brow. "Never mind that now. Besides your head, how do you feel?"

Her shaky hand found one of his. "Tired. Woozy. Also hungry."

A nervous chuckle scraped his throat. "We were cheated out of our date."

Her woozy eyes met his. "Date?"

His stomach flipped. "Our meal. You and I were meeting at the Italian restaurant for dinner. Remember?"

Her forehead creased and she shook her head, sucking in a breath and freezing before touching the bandage again. The movement must have hurt. "Tonight? I don't remember."

His whole body sank with the weight of that statement.

Vivi went to the other side and scanned Amelia's face. "You were in an alley behind the restaurant when the attack occurred. Can you tell us what happened? Did you see your attacker?"

"I don't... I can't..." her voice got quieter, tremulous again as she seemed to scan her memory.

"It's okay," Rory said even though it so fucking wasn't.

"What's the last thing you *do* remember?" Vivi asked gently.

Amelia started to shake her head again, stopped herself. Her gaze met Rory's. "You. Our session with the exercise bands."

He gave her hand a squeeze, even as his insides

cramped. He couldn't stop himself from looking at the psychologist, alarm bells ringing in his head.

"When was that?" Amelia asked him in a small voice.

He had to clear his throat before he could tell her. "Three days ago."

Vivi nodded, as if that were normal, and moved for the door. "Let me get Dr. Houston."

FOUR

T*wo days later*

DR. HOUSTON SIGNED the paperwork and removed it from his clipboard. "Here you go." He handed the papers to Amelia but Rory got to them first.

The doctor eyed him with a mix of irritation and patience. She did as well. Her guardian angel, as she had come to think of the gruff tech wizard, was mothering her to death, regardless of the fact she was feeling much better.

Except for a bit of memory loss, thanks to smacking her prefrontal cortex on the ground, and some wicked headaches that came out of nowhere but didn't last long. She was more than ready to leave the hospital.

Her attention flipped to the crutches waiting for her.

She dreaded having to use them, but if it got her out of here, she'd promise to skewer herself with them. "Thanks, doctor. I appreciate all you've done for me."

"Your script is waiting at the pharmacy. Remember RICE - Rest, Ice, Compression, and Elevation. The boot needs to stay on for six weeks, and then as long as everything heals correctly, you should be back to normal."

"And my head?"

He gave her a stoic smile. "The brain is an interesting phenomenon, and each one is unique. Your cognitive tests all check out and your systems appear perfectly healthy. Blood flow is good, electrical activity is normal, so I believe this is simply a reaction to the trauma and there's no long-term damage to your recall abilities. Try not to stress about it."

Easy for him to say. Not only did Rory, Beatrice, Vivi, and the police need to know what had happened and who did it, she herself feared what might happen if she *did* remember.

I shouldn't have been in that alley alone. At night, no less.

Hindsight was 20/20. *I should've had my stun gun in my hand and been more alert. I'm such a dummy.*

More than once she'd almost said all of that out loud to Rory and Vivi but knew they would argue with her, even if they secretly agreed. She'd gone over that day with both of them, as well as the detective in charge of her case—whom she could tell was overworked and had more important crimes than muggings to investigate—repeatedly, but nothing new had surfaced. It was just...blank.

Hannah and Jose had visited, hoping to spark something as well. The First Daughter's visit came with a lot of hoopla, including her bodyguards sticking close and sweeping the room for bugs. Amelia had exchanged a glance with Rory, rolling her eyes at Masden's thorough and unnecessary search, but she understood that stopping at the hospital wasn't exactly what the Secret Service agent wanted to be doing, either. The one thing that had flickered in the back of her mind was him—his insistence on protecting his charge with absolute efficiency.

Amelia had been happy to see Hannah and Jose, but that still hadn't jumpstarted her memory, even after the two of them described their interactions with her. Hannah had reminded her that she'd been equally annoyed by him the day of the mugging.

"Whatever you need," Hannah had said, "you let me know. And I'm getting you a new bag from Binni. I spoke to her this morning and told her what happened. She's bringing a replacement to the event Thursday night."

"She doesn't need to do that," Amelia had told her. "I have a backup, you know."

The First Daughter had waved it off. "She knows what a good friend you are to me and that you've been a supporter of her startup. I can't wait for the two of you to meet in person at the fundraiser. *If* you're able to come." She'd patted Amelia's arm, her own wrist wrapped with a brace. "I don't want you to overdo it, but if you feel like attending, I'll make sure you have whatever you need to be comfortable."

"I'll be there," Amelia had assured her, even when Rory grunted his disapproval. "A little mugging isn't going to stop me. I wouldn't miss it for the world."

Hannah had been thrilled, patting her hand before whisking Jose and the agents out of the room with promises of a wonderful dinner at the event.

Dr. Houston handed her a business card. "I'd like for you to consider seeing a colleague of mine. Dr. Thomas specializes in traumatic experiences. She's good."

Could therapy help her unlock her memories? "Got that covered," she told him, ignoring the card. "I've got my own therapist."

"Good. Not my area of expertise, but again I urge you to have counseling about the incident. Your brain appears to be in top condition, and this amnesia may be related to the emotional toll the assault had on you. Too often folks shrug this stuff off, try to be strong and ignore signs of stress, but violence is violence. It affects more than your physical body, and the memory loss could be the mind's mode of protecting itself. Think it over."

Rory tucked the papers away. "I'll be sure she gets what she needs."

He was worse than her parents. Amelia's poor mother and stepfather were heading home after their hurry to get here, seemingly as frustrated as Amelia that there was nothing further to be done. She needed time to recover, that was all, and apprehending the mugger was up to the police.

Her mother had offered to stay and take care of her while she was on the mend, but Amelia couldn't stand the idea of all three of them in her tiny apartment. Besides, there was nothing else wrong with her, headaches aside, and she wanted to get back to work. She could still instruct her patients from a chair, or on the crutches, and returning to SFI was the one thing she was looking forward to.

Dr. Houston nodded at Rory. "If you notice any extreme changes in her ability to focus, with her personality, or in her decision making, bring her back immediately." He held out a fist to her and she bumped it with her own. "I don't want to see you until your checkup. Stay off that foot."

After he exited, Rory patted the wheelchair's seat and grinned. "Nothing like getting a dose of your own medicine, huh, Doc?"

She contained her exasperation, refusing to let him get under her skin. Between the two of them, they got her situated in the chair. He'd removed the lower half of one leg of a pair of sweats since she couldn't get any of her yoga pants or slacks over the boot.

Her foot felt heavy and cumbersome, and it took Rory to help her get it on the metal footplate. "Don't get cocky on me," she warned. "This may slow me down but it certainly won't stop me."

He laid the crutches across her lap. "I have no doubt you'll be back to cracking the whip at all of us in no time."

Downstairs, her mother, stepfather, Beatrice, and Beatrice's husband, Cal, waited on the sidewalk in front of the entrance. A sleek black SUV was parked at the curb, and Connor waived from the driver seat while Cal retrieved the crutches and slid them into the rear compartment.

"I'm so glad they released you," her mother said, reaching for Amelia's hand.

Rory took the other and together they helped her

stand. She leaned against him, keeping her injured foot off the ground, but tried not to put too much weight on him, since he was still nursing his knee. Luckily, he seemed stable today, slipping an arm around her waist. "Me, too. Shouldn't you two be on your way home already?"

Her mother held tight, seemingly reluctant to release her. Her dark hair was shot through with silver, and her eyes had twice as many crow's feet as Amelia remembered. "Are you sure you don't want me to stay?"

What were the odds Hannah and the First Lady were doing a similar dance these days? "I appreciate you, Mom, but you know my place is too small, and you have a life to get back to." Her mother and stepfather had a dry cleaning business. They also babysat her sister's three young kids after school every day. Amelia knew them being here was a hardship on the rest of the family, and her sister needed them way more than she did. "I love you guys, and I'm glad you came to see me, but I'm fine, really."

"We'll take good care of her," Beatrice told them. "We consider her family."

Amelia's mother glanced at Rory and the arm he had around her daughter. "I can get a hotel room, if it's privacy you need."

"Mom!" Cheeks heating, Amelia released her mother's hands and fiddled with her hair. "Not appropriate," she muttered under her breath.

"What?" Her mother gave her a quelling look. "You didn't even tell us you had a boyfriend. If I stay, we can catch up. I can get to know Rory."

Amelia wished the sidewalk would open up and swallow her. She tried to straighten and put some distance between her and Rory. "As usual, you've totally read into things. He's my friend." She motioned at the gathered group. "They all are."

Rory stiffened. Cal opened the door to the backseat, acting like a bodyguard, and making a subtle gesture for her to get in.

"I love you, Mom." Careful to not lose her balance, she kissed her mother's cheek, and then accepted a kiss from her stepfather. While he could never take her own father's place, he'd been a good dad to her growing up. "You, too, David. I'll plan a trip home, soon. Meanwhile,"—she squeezed his arm—"take care of her for me, will you?"

Her mother acted offended, waving a dismissive hand in the air. "Please. He couldn't find the glasses on the end of his nose without me. If anyone needs taken care of, it's David."

The crowd shared a chuckle, David's robust laugh the loudest. "She's right." He put his arm around her mother's shoulders. "But I'll do my best, Ames."

No one but her family ever called her by that nickname, the sound of it bringing back a lot of memories, both good and bad. Her father had given it to her, but after his death, she'd refused to answer to it for many years. He'd been a kind, gentle, and quiet father, and they'd all been devastated at his loss.

A few years later when her mother had found David and a new chapter in her life, Amelia had acted out, becoming rebellious. Her teenage years had been a trial for all of them, enduring a particularly bad episode involving her and a friend nearly dying in a car crash. It had been David who'd reminded her that she wasn't the girl she'd become. She was her father's daughter—a sweet and caring soul who'd fallen through the cracks. While the dry cleaners didn't make much profit, he'd convinced her mother that Amelia needed grief counseling. It had saved her life.

Rory and Cal helped her into the backseat, Rory and Beatrice joining her there. Cal rode shotgun upfront with Connor. As they pulled away from the curb, she waved to her parents, seeing an orderly retrieve the wheelchair. David was still hugging her mother, and Amelia smiled. He, too, was a kind, gentle, and quiet man—except that belly laugh of his—and she owed him a great deal.

"You'll be staying at SFI," Beatrice announced. "We've already got a room on the third floor ready for you. It's small, but you won't be there long."

"That's not necessary." Seemed like she was saying that a lot the past few days, yet relief swam through her that she wasn't going to be alone in her apartment. The thought of that made her uneasy, as if the mugger might track her there and do even more harm.

Which was ridiculous, but there it was.

"It absolutely is," Beatrice argued. She and Cal, along with their daughter, spent all their time at SFI and were in the process of building a house at the new compound. They'd given their previous one to Dr. Montgomery and her husband, Ian.

'Musical houses,' Vivi had referred to it, and Amelia had wondered what it would be like to have her own. Not a cramped apartment or townhome, but a single family dwelling like she'd grown up in. Because of the fire that had taken her father's life, she'd always had mixed feelings about such a place, but found as she got older that she longed for one. Maybe even a yard, a spot for flowers, a garage to park a car in.

She'd dreamed about it plenty of times, and even done searches on a realtor app. A few months back, she'd attended several open houses, and then returned to her cramped apartment to create a Pinterest board with ideas, right down to flower boxes in the windows.

Pulling the trigger on buying one, however, hadn't happened. She had the money; it wasn't that. She'd thought by now she'd have a family like her sister, but her relationships hadn't worked out, and she was as devoted to her job as Cal, Beatrice, Rory, and the rest of the employees at Shadow Force. She lived and breathed helping others recuperate from their physical injuries, and she liked the staff and her patients.

Calling them friends was the truth—having Beatrice tell her parents that Amelia was family had made her heart swell with pride. They *were* a family—one based on common goals and interests rather than blood.

Besides, she didn't have the energy to worry about a bigger place, and she'd realized she probably wouldn't spend much time there anyway. Being independent was one thing; being alone was another.

Maybe I should get a cat.

"It'll make it easier for us to take care of you," Rory said, interrupting her train of thought and raising a hand to fend off her anticipated protest. His thigh was warm against hers. "And we all know that you're as capable as the rest of us, but like you've so often told me, every once in a while, we need a bit of help."

Amelia glanced at him, seeing the sly grin on his face. Once again, he was enjoying giving her a dose of her own medicine.

Thank goodness he hadn't taken offense with some of the things her mother had said and done. Yesterday, when Rory had given them some privacy, her mother had quizzed her about him. Amelia had explained that he was a patient, and she'd gone on and on about his amazing progress. Her mother had made a few polite comments, but seeing Amelia's excitement over him had leaned in and given her a chastising look. "He's a bit rough around the edges, isn't he?"

As fate would have it, the man in question had returned at exactly that moment, overhearing her mother's comment. Even now, thinking about it, Amelia felt heat rise in her cheeks. "You love that I'm a hobbled horse, don't you? Don't think for one moment I'm at your mercy."

"Never." They passed high-rises and Connor moved them smoothly from lane to lane, turning where necessary. The man next to her leaned in, lowering his voice. "I hate the fact you're in this predicament. Hate the fact that this happened, period. I'd give anything to go back and cancel our dinner so you were still walking around without a cast." Beatrice softly cleared her throat, as if reeling him away from the edge. He drew a deep breath and let it out slowly, and the wicked grin returned. "But having you at my mercy? Yeah, I can get used to that."

She'd known since she'd gained consciousness that this was eating him up. She didn't understand why he was blaming himself when it was her mistakes that had left her open to the attack. She bumped his elbow with hers. "You are not to blame for what happened."

He ignored the comment, shifting his attention to the passing scenery. "Your credit cards are cancelled and new ones have been issued. I reported your stolen driver's license to the DMV and you can get a new one as soon as you're up and about. The locks on your apartment doors have been changed, thanks to Moe, and we're keeping an eye out for any fraud or identity theft using your information."

He was all business again. In a way, that was good. "Any success catching the guy on video?"

His features hardened, his focus continuing to stay firmly on the direction they drove in. "It's like he knew where the cameras were and avoided them, but one of them caught him for a three-second shot. That's it. He was wearing black, had a hood over his head, and wore gloves. The frame is blurry and grainy due to the poor lighting. Moe and I have done everything we can to clear it up."

Beatrice confirmed it. "They've gone over each pixelated segment with a fine-tooth comb and shared the image with law enforcement. Unfortunately, there isn't much we've been able to gather from it to give us any identification of your mugger."

Thinking about that guy made her head hurt. "I really loved that bag," she said, rubbing her arm absentmindedly. "I wish I could remember more to help you."

"You will," Beatrice assured her.

"Meanwhile, once I have you at HQ again," Rory said, "Moe and I are hitting the streets to question as many people as we can about that night. Someone had to have seen something."

Traffic was light and they neared the multi-story building that blended in with all the others on this block, yet contained some of the most highly-trained military specialists in the world. It also held advanced technology and security that rivaled Hannah's. "Aren't the police doing that?"

He snorted. "Robberies and assaults happen a dozen times a day around here. The cops are overworked and understaffed like most cities. You are already yesterday's news and just another open case in a stack of them from this week alone."

Disappointment sat heavy in her stomach, but she was alive and that's what counted. She appreciated what Rory and Moe were about to do, but wished they'd leave it to the detective in charge. "So it sounds like you owe me a dinner," she said as they drove into the underground parking garage at SFI.

His demeanor instantly changed and he gave her a questioning look, his eyes now hid by the shadows. "I do, if you're still interested."

She grinned. "Tonight. Eight. My place or yours?"

He returned the smile. He lived in the basement next to the computer hub. The floor also contained the infirmary, gym, and her office. "You're the patient now. I'll order delivery and bring it to you."

"Good." She nodded, feeling her earlier anxiety lessen and a grin take its place. "Don't be late."

FIVE

Beatrice dug the end of her Mont Blanc pen into her blotter. Twirled it around and dug it in again.

Her two visitor chairs were filled, and Connor had brought in a third, forming a semi-circle on the other side of her desk. Parker, Moe, and Vivi sat waiting for her to sort through her thoughts and start their impromptu meeting while Rory settled Amelia into her room. Cal had Sloane, their daughter. Their dog, Maddy, napped on the girl's playmat in the far corner of the room. Maddy's snores rumbled softly in the background, reassuring and comforting.

Beatrice tossed down the pen and started with Parker. "You've reviewed her medical records?"

The doctor held a tablet and scrolled through the information on it. "Jax and I have gone over everything. The strike to the back of her head could have been far more serious. She's lucky to have walked away with only a concussion and short-term memory loss. We've reviewed the photos of the resulting contusion, but neither of us can draw a conclusion as to what the attacker used. The laceration was small, and like all head wounds, bled a lot, but was most likely caused from the blunt force trauma, not from a sharp edge."

"Could it be from a rock? Something our mugger found in the alley?"

"I can't rule that out, but a rock tends to have an irregular surface. The bruising suggests something more polished. All I know for sure at this point is that the attacker came from behind and walloped her. There are no defensive wounds because she didn't see it coming."

Moe tapped a thumb against his thigh, a nervous tick. "Show her what I found."

Parker tapped the screen and turned it so Beatrice could view it. "This was in the dumpster, along with the wooden end of a hammer, a busted lamp base, and broken glass and dishes, most likely from the restaurant. The pipe most closely matches the bruise. Sabrina has it in the lab, checking for Amelia's DNA, and our perp's fingerprints. It's a long shot, we know, but it's the best we've got. Other possibilities could include the butt of a handgun, a baseball bat...honestly, the list goes on and on. Without more information from Amelia herself, we're reaching." She glanced through her notes. "From the frame we have of our mugger, he looks to be approximately five-eleven, but even that is a guess. He could have taken the weapon with him, hiding it in his coat or in the purse."

Beatrice rocked gently in her chair, her mind working to re-create various versions of the scene with this new information. "Shooting her would've made too much noise, but hitting her in the back of the head was risky. The blow didn't immediately knock her out, and she may have seen him." It was that reason she had insisted on keeping Rory in Amelia's hospital room and two of her best bodyguards covertly stationed outside it. If their mugger realized she'd seen his face and could identify him, he might try to finish her off. *Overkill.* Again. *If* it was a simple purse snatching.

In Beatrice's world, nothing was ever simple or straightforward.

Moe lived in that same world. "Bloody coppers barely examined the alley and the dumpster."

"You did good." She took the tablet and used her fingers to blow up the photo of the metal pipe inside the evidence bag he'd placed it in before snapping the picture. "Approximately how long is it?"

"A third of a meter. Depending on the length of the asshole's arm"—he extended his own, demonstrating the strike—"he could've hit her from a meter back."

She did the conversion—the attacker could have struck Amelia from approximately three feet away. If he'd moved stealthily, he could have kept his presence a secret longer.

How many random muggers, coming up on a rare opportunity like this, could be so quiet *and* happen to have a piece of pipe on them for just such an occasion?

She didn't need her genius brain to calculate the odds. "Let's say he did keep that much distance between them. It would take a great deal of strength to hit her that hard with his arm fully extended."

Moe flipped his palms up toward the ceiling. "Either

that, or he moves like the wind and she didn't hear him when he got closer."

Vivi cleared her throat. "She might have been distracted, though. She was carrying on a text conversation with Rory, remember?"

Which brought up another anomaly. "Our perp didn't take her phone or jewelry, just the purse. Why?"

There was a short stretch of silence, then Vivi volunteered an answer. "There was something in it he wanted."

Parker shrugged. "Yeah, her wallet, cash, and credit cards. The keys to her place. He might not have realized she had the phone in her hand and believed it was in the bag."

Beatrice appreciated Parker playing devil's advocate, but she agreed with Vivi. "I think it's something more specific, more damning. The question is, what?"

"I questioned her about what she typically carries in her purse," the psychologist said. "She didn't mention anything unusual. Until she gets her memory back, we won't know for sure if she had something more important than her credit cards and lipstick in there. "And while I also assume it was a man, I recommend that at this point, we don't rule out anyone."

"Agreed. It could as easily be a female." Beatrice glanced at each of them in turn. "But we all agree, based on the inconclusive and insubstantial evidence we have, this was no random mugging."

All three nodded agreement without hesitation. "Something about it is off," Parker said, echoing Rory's words from the night of the mugging. "I try to be logical and stick with facts, not jump to conclusions and give into paranoia, put something isn't right about this."

Paranoia was common among them—Vivi had mentioned that fact more than once to Beatrice. But in the world of covert ops, survival depended on it. Being suspicious, overly cautious, and considering every scenario at all times, kept them safer.

She handed back the tablet. "We look at every angle and consider all possible scenarios. Create a timeline of everything Amelia did in the past two weeks, everyone she came into contact with, and why." She glanced at Moe. "I want to know everything about that piece of pipe, regardless if there are fingerprints or DNA on it. Our mugger could have wiped it down before he tossed it in the dumpster, hoping the contents would further hide or disguise any evidence."

He jumped to his feet, always ready for action. "I'm going to walk the route again and figure out how he disappeared so easily. Where he might've gone, as well as where he came from. Rory wants to go, too, but I'll ditch his ass before he can. Like he needs to hit the pavement with that knee of his. I'm due to take burgers and fries to some of the homeless in the area." One of their latest programs, thanks to Vivi, was picking up lunch at a fast food restaurant each day and hitting a different three block area around it to hand out meals. Any of the employees not on assignment took turns. Since a good many of the street people were veterans, it was a small way for SFI to give back. "I'll see if they've noticed anyone unusual lurking around."

She gave him a go-ahead nod and he headed for the door, Parker rising to her feet. She tucked the tablet under her arm. "With your permission, I'd like to interview Hannah. She and the driver were the last ones to see and speak to Amelia before this happened."

Beatrice had been thinking about that. The president's daughter was certainly high-profile and had plenty of admirers as well as enemies. She couldn't come up with one solid link from Hannah to the mugger, yet her brain wouldn't let go of the idea. "Let's not raise any suspicions at this point where it comes to her." If this involved the president or his family in any way, they could stir up a hornet's nest without realizing it, and that would put all of them in the wrong kind of spotlight. "Have Amelia put you in direct contact with Hannah under the guise of buying tickets for you and Moe to attend her fundraiser. From the dossier Rory gave me about the organization, Hannah has a penchant for helping kids of veterans. That's your in with her. Tell her you'd like to sponsor one —I'll front the grant money. Make it a kid who's interested in medicine and science. Try to befriend Hannah, find out what you can about her closest friends and advisors. We'll put their names into TrackMap, see what pops up."

The software program, developed by their founder, Emit Petit, was a people-mapping program that showed relationships between individuals and the groups they belonged to. She had often used a similar creation when she'd worked for Command and Control at NSA. They could link anything from human traffickers to digital hackers attacking the government.

Parker nodded and followed Moe out, leaving Vivi. "Can hypnosis help Amelia with her memory?" Beatrice asked.

"Sure." Vivi rose and went to pat the sleeping Maddy. "I can set up a session tomorrow if Amelia's game. Just to be clear, pushing her won't help and could actually set her back."

Maddy lazily cracked opened an eyelid, saw it was Vivi stroking her sleek, black hair, and went right back to sleep. "What are the odds of it doing that?"

Vivi chuckled. "You and your risk assessments. I can't give you a number."

"I'm good with a wild guess when it's coming from you."

The psychologist strolled to the door, massaging her neck and sending Beatrice a pointed look. Dr. Vivi Montgomery had one of the highest IQs Beatrice had ever encountered. "Our best bet is to focus on something besides the attack. The brain is an interesting and complicated instrument, making what would appear to be odd patterns and connections. Since she was texting with Rory when it happened, I'll use that relationship to attempt to spark her memory."

Smart. "Good." Beatrice retrieved her pen and doodled on the blotter. "Keep me updated."

"I know that look." Vivi paused at the door. "What could Amelia possibly have been carrying in her purse that this guy wanted? How would he even know?"

Beatrice didn't have the answer but she had her own assignment. "Jose, the driver, was the last person to see and talk to her, while she was in possession of her tote, right?"

Vivi followed her line of thinking. "And he's about the same height as our man in black."

"Exactly." Beatrice drew overlapping circles with Jose, Amelia, and Hannah's names in them.

"You think it's him?"

"I don't need TrackMap to show me the connection between him, Hannah, and Amelia."

"The police questioned him, and the traffic cams show he didn't leave his vehicle."

"I know," Beatrice admitted. There were holes in every theory she had, but there were also plenty of possibilities. "He could be working with someone."

"How would he know there would be a traffic jam? That Amelia would take off on foot?"

"I'm not saying he did, only that perhaps stealing her bag, and the contents thereof, wasn't a spur of the moment decision. If he had a clue about what she carried and also had an accomplice..." Beatrice shrugged. "I'm working through various scenarios."

"Have you forgotten Rory's possible connection to all of this?"

Beatrice glanced up. "I've considered it." The former assassin had more enemies than she did, both in the field, as well as in important government positions. Another potential hornet's nest. "I'm letting him look into those."

Vivi winked. "Gives him purpose. Something to focus on and not wallow in helplessness."

"Keeps him from self-detonating," Beatrice added.

"You would have made a decent psychologist."

She laughed and sat back. It was time to find Cal and Sloane and enjoy a family dinner. "I'll leave that to you, Dr. Montgomery."

Vivi offered a gracious bow. "Do me a favor?"

"Sure, anything."

She gave Beatrice a knowing once-over. "Don't be like Rory and decide you're at fault for this."

"Why would I?"

"You and Rory are alike in that way—you blame yourself for far too many things. You weren't to blame for your mother taking her own life. Not to blame for Rory being temporarily paralyzed and choosing to stay in the wheelchair far longer than he needed to. When I first met you, your emotional quotient was one of the lowest I'd seen, mostly because you'd had a rough time with your mother and you'd shut down feeling anything for anybody. Since I've worked here, I've noted that it's risen considerably. You've created your own family and that's the best medicine ever, but you take what happens to each of them personally, even when you know you can't control outside conditions."

Especially then. *Illogical.* She knew that, but it didn't change anything. She could be as illogical as she wanted when it came to the people she loved. "Sometimes you're too smart for your own good, Doctor. No offense to your profession, but honestly, all the hours I spent in therapy talking about my childhood didn't do me any good."

Vivi nodded, acknowledging it. The gleam in her eye suggested she thought that she could have helped, though. "What did?"

Beatrice couldn't help but smile as she remembered Cooper Harris and her stint in San Diego. "I sort of fell into a family with the SCVC Taskforce with Cal, Rory, and Emit during an operation that turned into a goatfuck. It's how Rory ended up in that wheelchair." The memories of that night—of seeing the violence wrought—were etched forever in her brain. "Each of them, that team, made me a better person because they gave me hope, allowed me to believe in the goodness of people again. I learned to trust them to have my back, to lift me up when I needed it, not beat me down farther."

"And you've taken that and made it a key component for SFI." Vivi offered a thumbs up. "You've done good, B."

Beatrice smiled even broader. "We're just getting started."

SIX

Rory tucked Amelia into bed in the sparse room as soon as they'd landed. The place hadn't been used in a while, but someone had brought a plant and hung a serene landscape on the wall. It had taken some maneuvering to get her into a comfortable position between the boot and her sensitive neck. Finally, they'd found the best combo of pillows to pad her head and elevate her leg.

She'd asked him to stay until she fell asleep, then acted embarrassed by the request. He'd reassured her that he'd stay until she kicked him out if she wanted, and she'd gathered her courage and insisted he leave. "I'll be fine."

He'd countered. "It's normal to feel out of sorts after an attack and to hate the idea of sleep. We're most vulnerable then. Besides, I'd like to stay for a few minutes, just to be sure you don't need anything."

While she'd tried to keep up her bravado, he'd seen the

relief in her eyes. She'd instantly fallen asleep once he'd sat next to the bed, and that was good—she needed rest.

He'd been too keyed up, though. Down in the gym, he'd ran through a punishing leg workout that had his knee barking in pain.

Good. The new injury had fired up his entire leg and lower back. Montgomery thought his disability was mostly in his head—he would put that to the test.

The grueling workout might set back his recovery, but it had at least cleared his mind. Emotions he didn't normally let surface had been front and center since the attack. He kept reliving the fear and anger he'd experienced, seeing Amelia lying face down in that alley. Felt his inability to get to her without resorting to crawling.

Fuckin A. If he had to crawl, so be it. He'd do it all over again.

The helplessness it had generated was not easy to overcome. He hadn't felt so, dare he even think it, *impotent*—god, he hated that word—since he'd taken those two bullets to his spine and woken up in a hospital, his legs paralyzed. The debilitating back pain and endless consults with experts, who'd assured him it would simply take time and physical therapy to regain his strength and mobility, had created a deep well of anger that had never been extinguished. He'd tried for a while to hold onto hope. Mostly for Beatrice because she was so damned bullheaded and kept insisting he could reinvent himself as she'd done.

That was a pipe dream. He'd been a lot of things in his life, took on the role of many different personas when undercover. So many, in fact, he wasn't sure he even knew who he really was.

Propping up his leg on a nearby stool, he let go of a bit of the tension in his shoulders and touched his keypad. Stupid thing brought him comfort. From here, he could control everything, unlike outside these walls.

His bat cave, as he referred to it, was a semi-circular desk with multiple screens, phones, and a single toy figurine—Batman. The character had been a hero to him as a boy and he'd strived to be like the fictional champion. Moving in the shadows, conquering evil, bringing justice to those in need.

Dusting off the masked toy, he realized he, too, needed to clean up. Not just a shower and a change of clothes, but his mind. He'd neglected that anger, those buried emotions, always close to the surface. Everything was all tangled up. Rory hated chaos.

He massaged his knee and grimaced. It was swelling again and needed ice.

The refrigerator in Ops was the size of a stamp and didn't have an ice maker. If he wanted a compress, he'd have to head to the med ward and that meant seeing Jax. The man had already sent multiple texts, inquiring about his knee.

He switched from massaging that to his low back, inflating the lumbar support pillow in his chair. Pain, anger—they went hand in hand. If only he could get rid of one or the other, maybe he could be normal again.

Who was he kidding? He'd never aspired to be normal. He wanted to be a goddamn hero.

Again.

His computer screens were dark—he hadn't been here since everything went down—and for a brief moment, he didn't know where to start.

And wasn't that a revelation in itself?

The elevator dinged and he mentally groaned when Vivi Montgomery walked out, carrying a tray.

She saw his frown and grinned. Pure evil, that one. "Don't act like I'm your worst nightmare. I brought you a topical pain reliever, coffee, and my services. Where do you want me to start?"

"You're not touching my leg," he growled.

"Let me rephrase—my *tech skills*. I have no intention of playing nursemaid beyond handing you some aspirin and refilling your coffee."

Pure evil with a heart of gold. Was that possible? He'd wanted time alone, but God knew he needed to think and he hadn't been able to for the past few days. Vivi knew when to talk and when to leave him to his thoughts. Usually. "Beatrice sent you, didn't she?"

"I come of my own volition. Now, do you want this stuff or not?"

Without waiting for his reply, she slid the tray onto the desk. There was even a cold pack in a stretchy knee brace. He reached for that first and sighed, draping it over the swelling. Ignoring the self-satisfied look on her face, he guzzled half the coffee—perfect temp as always and from her personal stash—and cocked his chin toward the cubicle she often used. "Look into recent muggings in the area. Pinpoint those with assaults and run background checks on the suspects in open cases and those arrested on the others, if they're out on the streets again." Busywork. It would keep her out of his hair and away from stumbling on potential landmines. "Print any that tickle your big brain and throw them into TrackMap with Amelia."

She nodded and sat, waking the computer.

He focused on the three blank screens in front of him, listening to the quiet click of her fingers on the keyboard. He wished he could search Amelia's apartment, but that was out of the question at the moment since he could barely stand. Ashamed of his physical weakness, he texted Moe, telling him he'd decided his skills were needed here, at HQ, and Moe could have the grunt work of walking the streets and interviewing folks.

Cush life, you got there, mate, was Moe's reply. *You owe me.*

He sent back a rude emoji, but at least the bastard hadn't offered pity or worry about Rory's physical state.

For now, he had a rabbit hole to dive into, and he needed to come up with an idea for tonight's dinner.

Chasing bad guys? Easy. Impressing Amelia without a fancy restaurant to back him up? *Kill me now.*

Booting up his computer, he forced his emotions into the anger hole so he could detach and keep his head as clear as possible. Vivi's presence might actually be good. He had to stay on guard around her.

Setting the timer on his phone, he placed a silent bet with himself that she'd stay quiet twenty minutes and then she'd find a way to engage him in conversation. Too clever for her own good, she'd start by showing him something innocuous in her research and the next thing he'd know, she'd trick him into facing his *feelings* about the incident.

Fuck that. Studying human behavior wasn't only for

psychologists. He'd been a SEAL, a spy, an assassin. For a brief moment, he stared at the back of her head, pretending he could see inside it as he ciphered through the list of data he'd gathered about her. Her only weak spot was her husband. Like all humans, she would do anything to protect those she loved, and while Ian Kincaid was over six feet of solid SEAL himself, and didn't need protecting, she was a rabid dog about him. If she even tiptoed into the feelings department, he'd bring up Ian's next assignment.

For the first time since the guy had joined SFI, he was going on a true undercover training assignment. Parker, head of their Covert Ops team, was sending him with Ryker Baptiste and Mia Shane to Germany on a weekend hands-on tutorial to learn about the art of spy craft.

Not that Rory could share details, but...he could taunt Vivi with them.

Hehehe.

She lasted twenty-three minutes. The printer had spit out a few pages, but she was still typing away and reading what her searches brought up when she asked, "What if our mugger simply wanted that handbag, not the contents?"

He was knee-deep in a dark web forum where local criminals came to boast about their offenses. He hadn't come across any postings that sounded like Amelia's assault and robbery, but he'd found a thread of someone asking about it. No one had claimed responsibility, which tended to be because it was a street person or non-career criminal who didn't know about these shadowy groups, or they didn't want to admit to what they'd done. No one seemed to know any facts about it either, meaning whoever had committed the crime hadn't bragged on the street. "Already checked local pawn shops," he told her, frustrated. "Nada."

"Did you check eBay and the other online resale sites?"

"I put flags on all of them. If that bag goes up for sale anywhere in the world right now, I'll get a notification."

She tossed a smile over her shoulder at him. "They don't call you Mr. Computer Wiz for nothing."

"No one calls me that. If they did, I'd kill them."

"Which is why they don't say it to your face, Wiz," she countered with a wink, "but they *do* behind your back."

He eyed Batman. "I'm not discussing how I feel about what happened."

She rolled her chair away from her desk to face him. "I didn't ask you to."

"Sure you did. You're buttering me up so I'll spill my guts."

"What do you need to spill your guts about? Unless this tripped a trigger? I thought we'd covered everything in therapy."

And there it was—that backdoor way of hers to slip in and get him talking. "We could have sessions for the next hundred years and never cover all of my failures and faults."

"Hmm." She shrugged and scooted back to her keyboard.

That was it? He frowned at his screen, finding it hard to concentrate now. She'd let him off too easily. "What I need is an idea for dinner."

"We have a cafeteria."

"Amelia has called in her raincheck. I need something nicer than a microwave meal."

Spinning again, she faced him but stayed at the desk, delight clear on her face. "That's great! It's probably better if she doesn't go anywhere right now, though, don't you think?"

He started a new search. This one for delivery places. "She's not up for going out. I mean, what should I order *in* for us? Should I stick with Italian?"

Amusement lit her eyes. "Why don't you make something?"

He snorted. "I can't cook."

"All those years on your own and you never learned to put a meal together?"

"Is there some underlying diagnosis you want to throw out about that?"

Her laughter was infectious. He had to school his features not to smile. "You're a trip, Rory. I don't spend every minute of every day analyzing what you tell me, you know."

Sure she did. Just like analyzing situations was second-nature to him, scrutinizing, probing, and dissecting every habit, belief, and personality trait was to her.

His coffee was lukewarm. He finished off the last of it and rubbed his eyes. He needed sleep, but at least the throbbing in his knee would keep that at bay. He didn't want to order from the same restaurant, so he scanned a list of others in the neighborhood. All claimed they would deliver.

But...that was a bad idea. Beatrice didn't like outsiders

showing up at the front entrance. Maybe he could bribe Connor or Moe to pick something up?

He shot off texts to each, crossing his fingers that one would do him a solid.

"Beatrice has Moe and Parker working on this," Vivi volunteered, "but if there's anything I can do specifically for you? Take you somewhere, investigate for you? I'm game."

"You need to stay in your comfy office and let those of us who are qualified handle it."

She blew a raspberry. He sensed her desire to argue, but she didn't, surprising him once again. "What time is your dinner?"

He checked the clock. "An hour."

"It's Saturday night, Rory. No one is going to be able to put together a meal for pickup or delivery that fast."

Shit. He hadn't thought of that. Running a hand through his hair, he swore under his breath. "Maybe she'll be too tired to eat."

Vivi stood, shut down her monitor and waved for him to follow. "Come on."

He eyed her as she walked to the elevator. "No."

"Yep." She punched the button. "Let's go see what we can make for her."

Fuck. He hung his head, knowing he was in a no-win situation. He would not bail on Amelia, and he'd promised dinner. Once again, he found himself outmaneuvered by the woman holding the elevator doors for him. "I can't," he lied, pointing to his knee. "Afraid my ass is stuck here for a while."

"Afraid is right. They'll be calling you Chickenshit,

rather than Wiz. I'll get your wheelchair." She sounded entirely too happy about it. "You have to get up eventually."

He practically knocked his travel mug over coming to his feet. "No." He was never going back to that blasted thing. "Just give me a damn minute, all right? I'm coming, but don't think that I don't know what you're doing."

She grinned like the Cheshire Cat again. "As long as you're up and walking, I don't give a damn."

Downstairs in the kitchen, they hunted through cabinets and the giant commercial refrigerator, coming up with a variety of ingredients, but no inspiration about what to make. Rory leaned on the counter, ignoring his throbbing knee. "I should just cancel."

Vivi shot him a dismayed look. "You will not, Chicken."

"Give it up, doc. You're not going to goad me into this."

At that moment, he was saved from her blistering argument when their head cook, Kimico, hustled in. Less than five feet, her dark hair short and graying, she narrowed her eyes at them before she spoke in broken English. "What you two doing in my kitchen?"

Vivi smiled at the petite Japanese woman, but Rory thought she should take a step back since Kim was carrying a large meat cleaver. "Dr. Thorpe is staying with us for a few days, maybe longer. She's been living on hospital food, so we came to fix dinner for her."

Kim wiggled the knife. "I make her something."

Rory rounded up some courage. "Can I help? I owe her a meal."

The cook ran her gaze over him and must've found him worthy of her space. Setting down the knife, she grabbed a loaf of Texas toast and tossed it to him. "She like grilled cheese. Add tomato, lots of mayonnaise."

"I can handle that."

Kim put the cleaver away. "On your own?"

"Yes," he ground out, forcing a smile.

"Don't leave mess in kitchen." Then she left.

Rory breathed a sigh of relief. "Ironic."

"What?" Vivi asked.

"My grandmother always had a garden and did her best to get me to eat vegetables. My favorite food when I was seven was grilled cheese, and she would sneak tomato and cucumber into them." He chuckled. "Even as an adult, I don't particularly like vegetables."

"Why doesn't that surprise me?" She went to work gathering the butter and cheese. "Let's rehearse your questions."

"Don't need to," he lied.

She handed him a fry pan, spatula, then rooted around until she found a stack of plates, pulling out two. "The script is the key. Isn't that what you always say?"

It was a technique he'd learned when he was in the SEALs. Every mission, he would create a flow chart, mapping out the different things that *could* happen and what response his team would take if they did. He'd also used it frequently during undercover operations. "What about it?"

"It's clear you're still nervous about having dinner with her. So let's review the questions we came up with in our last session and script it out in this new environment."

He dropped a chunk of butter in the pan. "I'm scrapping those questions and starting with something else."

Vivi grabbed a cutting board and pulled a tomato from the fridge. "Okay." The tone in her voice told him she thought that was a bad idea, but she would play along. "Hit me with it."

"I need to put her at ease—this potential relationship is fragile, especially now." How was that for psychoanalyzing someone. "I'm going to start by asking about her parents. She seems close to them. That should break the ice."

Vivi tried to hide her grin, but he saw it. "I think that's perfect."

He had two sandwiches in the pan coming along nicely when Ian showed up. He and Vivi greeted each other with light kisses and knowing smiles, and Rory pretended not to notice.

After a moment, Ian turned to him, still holding Vivi's hand. "I'm wheels up in two hours, heading to Chicago to meet Ryker and Mia before we're on to Germany. I need your advice."

"Leave your personal devices here and take a sterile phone only. When you return, remove the battery and bring it to me. At the hotel, obtain a room on a middle floor, between the second and sixth, and be sure you have a doorstop with you. Know all the exits, and keep your doors locked at all times. The rest your mentors will walk you through before you leave the States."

Ian nodded, kissed his frowning wife, and patted Rory's shoulder. "Thanks, man."

Once he was gone, Vivi asked, "How did you know that's what he was talking about?"

"He had the look."

"What look?"

"Men get it when they're focused on the mission ahead of them."

"Women, too?"

"Some."

Rory held up a hand to stave off her impending interrogation. "Sandwiches are ready." He slid one onto each plate. "Can you bring me a tray and two waters?"

"He'll be safe, right?"

The guarded fear in her eyes was real. After what they'd been through recently, Rory couldn't blame her. "The tadpole is in good hands. It's only a training exercise."

"Right." She gathered what he needed and walked with him to the elevator. "Enjoy your dinner. I'll clean up."

In his head, he was already scripting like she'd suggested. She really was a good psychologist. "He's a good man and has natural instincts. You can't teach that. He's going to make a hell of a spy."

Her shoulders relaxed, and she smiled at him as the elevator doors began to close. "Be charming," she called.

Oh, he would be. He was going to charm the hell out of Amelia.

SEVEN

The clock was ticking down to the golden hour on the wall clock, *tick tick tick*. Amelia's pulse skipped along with it.

This room had to be in demand—it was one of the few that had an en suite bath. She checked her appearance in the tiny bathroom mirror and found it appalling.

When she'd woken from her nap thirty minutes ago, she was sweating, her head throbbed, and she'd stumbled to the toilet just in time to vomit there rather than the floor.

Small miracles.

Once she'd stopped seeing three vanities, she'd splashed water on her face, then caught a whiff of body odor with a side of hospital bed *eau de awful*. Time for a shower. Some good Samaritan had placed bottles of shampoo and body wash on the edge of the tub.

Knowing she was still recovering from a concussion, she'd debated if doing anything alone was wise, especially getting in and out of the stall. Sitting on the toilet seat, she'd considered who to call. Tricky question, that.

Stomach rumbling at its emptiness, she'd ignored the crutches and cruised the pieces of furniture to the small kitchenette. There, she'd gulped some water, ate the saltine crackers her Samaritan had left her, and felt...not quite so bad.

In fact, she'd felt almost normal. Scratch that. Not normal, but better than she had earlier. While she'd found it impossible to sleep in the hospital with all the noise on the floor, and the constant coming and going of nurses and aides to check on her, the nap must have done her good.

The sweating had abated and her stomach had finally settled. She'd finished another glass of water, noticed her vision no longer made her feel drunk, and tested walking around more, careful to keep weight off her foot.

The good thing was, she hadn't been dizzy, light-headed, or nauseous. She'd sorted through a pile of clothes left on a chair near the door and grimaced at the bland, generic items. They were clean, at least, and smelled of detergent, rather than sick people.

The doctor had ordered her to keep the boot on and only take sink baths. Finagling that seemed harder than stepping into the shower, however. She'd found an unused plastic bag for the waste can and enclosed her leg inside that, boot and all, and secured a knot at the top.

There were bars on the shower walls that helped her stay steady. The heat had relaxed her tight shoulders and the body wash smelled like lemon and eucalyptus. She took her time, allowing the water to sluice over her sore muscles, keeping the back of her head and neck out of the stream.

Her textured hair could use a day at the salon, but that would have to wait. She'd have to skip washing it for now, but maybe Vivi or Sabrina would assist tomorrow.

All the effort had caught up with her and she'd felt a bit shaky. She'd moved to the bed to dress in the casual T-shirt and sweatpants provided.

Too bad she'd seen her ashen face in the mirror. Her first date with Rory was only minutes away and she looked like she was three feet from her grave.

Beatrice had a beauty drawer in her desk filled with makeup, hand cream, nail polish, and assorted perfumes. The head of SFI was tough as nails, but balanced her badass self with a love for girly things. Best of all, she made no bones about it.

Amelia was about to text her and ask to borrow mascara and lip gloss when there was a knock at the door.

"Amelia Bedelia," Sabrina, their lab tech and all around upbeat coworker, sang. "Just checking on you, girl. You all right in there? You need anything before your date?"

How does she know? Amelia was grinning as she hopped over to the door and found the flamboyant redhead standing there with Amelia's overnight suitcase in one hand and a garment bag slung over her shoulder. "Tell me that's all for me."

Sabrina pointedly looked her over from head to toe. "Damn girl, you look like shit."

The one thing Amelia really adored about Sabrina, besides her always bright disposition, was the fact she called things as they were. "Feel like it, too. Although, I'm getting better. Being here helps."

Sabrina set the items on the bed before she dug around inside the overnighter and came out with Amelia's bright pink makeup bag. "Bathroom, now." She pointed. "We've got serious work to do and not much time to get it done."

The two joked and laughed as Sabrina applied foundation, blush, and eyeliner. Within minutes, Amelia found her reflection appeared almost normal. When she slipped into the soft cotton skirt that fell well below her knees and the matching blouse from her wardrobe, she hugged her friend and heaped oodles of gratitude on her. "How did you know about the date?"

Sabrina winked, tucking the suitcase in the small closet and handing Amelia a pair of leather slip-ons. "I have my spies," she declared. "Plus, Beatrice asked me to go to your place and pick up a few things. Trace is still guarding it, just in case, but so far, no one has shown up."

"Well, that's a relief. Hopefully, the mugger is happy with what he got and doesn't try to raid my place on top of it."

"You're sure there was no one stalking you?"

She'd been asked that question already, and yet, it still hit her as odd. "It was a random attack. I'm just a physical therapist, I'm not well known or anything."

"*Just?*" Sabrina looked offended. "You got the curmudgeon known as Rory on his feet and walking. That's a historical feat. You should get a medal."

She laughed. "I'm not sure he would agree with you, and I admit that I've had a few patients claim I'm a sadist when I've pushed them during therapy, but I don't have any enemies. I'm not…"—she almost said, *special like the rest of you*, but cut off the words—"interesting. No offense, but because of the types of lives you've all led, you see a conspiracy around every corner. You think there's more to everything than there actually is."

Sabrina gave her a half-hearted smile. "You're right. We do. We walk around looking over our collective shoulders, but we have good reason for it. Be patient. We're all worried about you. Sometimes people who love you need something to focus on. Conspiracy theories are an excellent distraction."

Love? On one hand, she appreciated it. It was sweet that they were so concerned about her well-being and convinced they needed to keep her safe. On the other, the questions freaked her out. "I know. Give me a few days and I'll be back to normal. We'll put all of this behind us. Beatrice—as well as the rest of you—have better things to worry about than me."

"I only brought a few days' worth of clothes. Hopefully, you can go home before you run out of underwear, but I'm happy to pick up more, and you can always use the washer and dryer downstairs. If you need help—"

"I know, call you." She motioned her to the door. "Thanks again. I can't tell you how much better I feel."

In the hall, Sabrina glanced back. "You and Rory, huh? I'd say you're pretty interesting."

Amelia felt her cheeks heat. "Under that scruffy beard and cavalier attitude, he's such a good man."

As if she'd conjured him, the elevator doors opened and there he stood with a tray in hand. Sabrina braced a foot against one panel to keep them open, and he barely glanced at her, eyes glued on Amelia.

"Damn." He limped toward her, and she couldn't keep the smile off her face, thinking about the two of them hobbling around together. "You look amazing. I didn't know we were dressing up."

Over his shoulder, Sabrina winked and the doors closed. Amelia gingerly shifted out of Rory's way and ushered him inside. "Sabrina brought me a few of my things. Here." Using it for balance, she slid the extra chair around to the tiny table near the window to create a seating area for them. "Is that grilled cheese I smell?"

"My culinary skills are limited." He set down the tray and helped her into the chair. "But these babies have my special sauce on them. Prepare for your taste buds to be captivated."

She chuckled, helping him arrange the food and drinks. He'd even remembered napkins.

Suddenly starving, she dove in, skipping any pretense of making polite conversation first. She laughed at herself when sauce ran down her fingers and she sucked it off rather than using a napkin. "This beats hospital food any day. What kind of cheese is this?"

He stared at her as if he couldn't quite believe the gusto with which she'd attacked the simple sandwich. She couldn't believe it herself. "A mix of cheddar and Colby-Jack. Super rare and fancy," he joked.

"How did you know I love tomatoes on my sandwiches?"

"A little bird told me. One with a very big meat cleaver and an attitude."

She found herself giggling. "Kim let you in her kitchen?"

He puffed out his chest. "All I had to do was turn on the Tephra charm."

"You didn't bully her to death, did you?"

Offended, he turned defensive. "Would I do such a thing?"

She snickered and continued eating. It was just so good.

When she finished the last bite, she noted he was still staring at her with a bit of awe on his face. He was only halfway through his sandwich, but he wiped his fingers and handed her a bottled water. "You need to stay hydrated."

She accepted it, downed half, and then sighed with relief over her full belly. "My mother always claims food tastes better if it's been prepared by someone who—" she caught herself right before she said *loves*. "Someone who cares for you."

His bushy brows lifted ever so slightly, and then he glanced down at his remaining sandwich. "Sounds true to me."

So he did care for her, right? God, she felt like a four-teen-year-old high school girl, trying to catch an older boy's attention. Now that she had it, she was all kinds of flustered.

Granted, she'd had few relationships in her lifetime. For the most part, she's always been a quiet, introverted geek. In college, she preferred to stay in her dorm room and study, rather than go out and party with friends. By the time she was in grad school, she didn't really have many. She'd always been more devoted to her studies and learning than socializing.

Which...now made her feel as awkward as could be. It was one thing to talk with patients during sessions, easing their stress and encouraging them about their rehab. Alone with Rory was as opposite of that as you could get.

He cleared his throat. "Your mom and stepdad seem nice."

She fiddled with her napkin, creasing it in half and then half again. "They are. I'm lucky to have them."

"And your biological father?"

Although he never talked about himself, Rory knew everyone's background—it was part of his job. He helped Beatrice recruit employees, making sure they were a good fit for SFI. She assumed he knew the details of the fire that had killed her dad and destroyed their home. Yet, she understood he wasn't asking for facts surrounding her dad's untimely death, but rather her relationship with him.

The memories were bittersweet. "I was nine when he died, but he was my whole world. When I lost him... I lost a piece of me." She shook herself out of the melancholy. "You would've liked him. He was an electrician, but he tinkered with things. All kinds of gadgets. Computers, phones, radios, and TVs. Had a big workbench, dozens of his projects strewn everywhere. Drove my mom crazy. I loved it—it was like hidden treasure. He could take pieces and parts from a bunch of things and put them together to create something new. I always wanted to be able to do that." She shrugged. "Anyway, he taught me all kinds of random stuff, like a modern MacGyver. He knew Norwegian, of all things, and how to solder metal. He showed me how to make pasta from scratch and how to hot wire a car." Rory laughed and she nodded. "He took karate and taught me this self-defense move where you—"

Her mind went blank, then there was a flash. Shoes. She saw her favorite sneakers in her lap. She was in the backseat of a car, it was night.

"Amelia?"

Her head snapped up. She was sweating again. Using a fresh napkin, she dabbed at her hairline. "Sorry. What was I saying?"

Rory studied her with more intensity, his dinner forgotten. "About your dad teaching you self-defense."

"Right." She twisted the napkin. Her mind seemed to blank out again as she tried to recall what she was about to say. It was like waking from a dream that seemed real but faded so fast you couldn't remember it.

Her stomach clenched, another sliver of memory rose unbidden—a dark alley, the sound of footsteps. She reached for the back of her skull, pain making her gasp. "Rory?" Her voice trembled.

He was beside her in an instant. "What is it? Do you need to lay down?"

She lifted her gaze to his. "I think I..."

Another shockwave hit—this time behind her eyes. She cried out and pitched forward, all sense of balance gone.

He caught her, managing to lift her into his arms. Cradling her, he limped his way to the bed and laid her down gently. "It's okay. Deep breaths. I'll get Jax."

She grabbed his forearm, holding on for dear life. "Don't leave me."

He bent over her. "I'm right here. I'm not going anywhere. But I need to alert Jax. Take you to the infirmary."

"No. Just give me a minute, please?" Already she felt more stable. The pain was ebbing. "The pills." She pointed to the dresser where an orange bottle sat.

Rory brought one and the remaining water to her. He helped her sit so she could swallow it. The room didn't spin, nor did she see three of him, and she breathed a sigh of relief. "Headache—that's all. I'm fine now."

"I'll call Jax."

She would not ruin their date again, dammit. "Sit with me for a minute first." She patted the edge of the mattress. "Please?"

His eyes were hard, his movements reluctant, but he did as she asked, his weight dipping the bed so she tipped, knocking her shoulder into his. She left it there and he put an arm around her. "We should have postponed this," he said. "You need to rest."

That was the last thing she needed. Her skirt was tangled around her legs, revealing far more than it should. She adjusted the fabric, feeling him tense beside her. "What I need is for everyone to not baby me. I will recover from this, and yes, it's going to take a bit of time but I'll be right as rain soon. I've survived worse."

The worry in his eyes lessened. "I like your style, you know."

He was so close, so solid. It felt good to lean against him. "I like yours, too."

For a brief heartbeat, she thought he'd kiss her, but then he cleared his throat, glanced away, and pushed to his feet. "I'm still taking you to the infirmary. You shouldn't be alone."

When he tried to scoop her up, she smacked his arms and shifted back. "I just got out of the hospital. I'm not returning to an uncomfortable bed and a fussing doctor."

Rory put his hands on his hips, eyes hard again. "After what just happened here, you are not spending the night alone."

"Then stay with me."

His lips moved but nothing came out. He blinked slowly. "You want me to...?" He shook his head. "I have to be in Ops in case... Well, one of our newest members is on a training mission in the field and I need to be available, you know, in case anything goes wrong."

"I'll come down there, then. I don't mind. I can sleep on your couch."

He looked like a deer caught in headlights. "You will not. I'm taking you to Jax. You'll be under his care and carefully watched, and—"

"No." He blinked again at her sharp word said a bit louder than she'd planned on. She lifted her chin. "I'm spending the night with you."

For a laughable moment, he did that lip moving thing again, then he regrouped, nodded, glanced around. He fiddled with his hands and went to her closet, snatching up the suitcase. "Has anyone ever told you you're a PITA?"

She grinned. "I never used to be." Quiet, geeky Amelia never raised her voice to anyone. "Guess I learned everything I know in that manner from you. Now, let's go."

EIGHT

What the hell was he doing, bringing Amelia to his room? Not only was his personal quarters a complete disaster, he didn't know the first thing about taking care of her.

Sure, he'd had field medical training back in the day, but concussions were unpredictable.

Plus, now he had to be charming for longer than an hour or two.

I'm so screwed. If she was around him for long, she'd see the real Rory Tephra.

And she wouldn't like it.

No one did. That was his strategy—keep everyone at arm's length.

The elevator dinged and opened to the basement floor and the Ops center. Down the hall to the left was the medical ward, to the right was the enormous indoor gym and physical therapy center.

"I should run to my office," Amelia said, peeking longingly in that direction, "and grab some files. Everyone's sessions have been put on hold while I was gone. Now that I'm back, I can oversee them. I need to check my planner and rearrange next week's schedule."

He admired her willpower, and while he started to argue, he also knew it might take her mind off the attack. He had a shit-ton of work waiting for him, and he certainly wasn't going to let his busted knee stop him from diving in. Giving her any quarter was probably a bad idea, but on the other hand, it would give her something to do for the next few hours while he sorted through the tasks waiting for him. "On one condition."

The lights had been out and they automatically came on as the two of them entered into his territory. She faced him, hugging the crutches and crossing her arms over her chest. "What?"

She looked far too pale under the LEDs. He needed to cart her off to Jaxon and assure himself she was in the best care. Let her be pissed all she wanted.

But he remembered what it was like to be an invalid. To be lying in bed with people waiting on him and asking every few minutes how he was feeling. He knew how it felt when your body wouldn't cooperate and your mind was in overdrive. It was best to play along, get her off her feet, and give her something to focus on. "Every thirty minutes, you take a break. If you start feeling dizzy, sick to your stomach, or you experience blurry vision, you tell me immediately. I'll get you comfortable at a cubicle and we can bring up your online calendar so you can reschedule your patients, but that's all. Once you're done with that, I'm putting you to bed. No arguments."

She opened her mouth, snapped it shut. He could see the cogs in her head turning behind her glare as she weighed her options. "I'll agree to your terms if you agree to mine."

"Yeah?" She was going to regardless, but again, he had enough sense to play along and make her *think* she was in charge. His experience leading a SEAL team had taught him a lot back in the day, and one of the best things he'd learned was to make every member feel valued and seen. A team was only as strong as its weakest link, and being in a group of elite warriors every bit as trained and intelligent as him, it had only made sense. Looking at the determined woman in front of him, he knew he needed to apply the same tactic.

"Yeah. Are you scared?"

Amelia had an equal amount of experience and intelligence in her field, and he needed to respect that she would tell him if she felt sick or needed rest. Yes, she would push herself to her limits, but she would finally admit when she couldn't do anymore. "Of you? Please. What's your condition?"

She pointed at his knee. "You take a break with me after every thirty minutes and we both put our feet up."

Like that would be a hardship. Although his legs were trembling with exertion, he was enjoying the verbal sparring with her. "I'm fine and I don't have a concussion."

She moved faster than he could have anticipated, giving him the gentlest of shoves. While his core was strong from all the workouts he did, his legs couldn't take the sudden shift, and his knee screamed in pain. He nearly toppled to the ground.

Thank God his reflexes were still decent. Dropping her suitcase, he shot out both hands and connected with the set of wooden cabinets running the length of the wall to keep from landing on his ass. He bumped the blinds and the stupid things banged into each other, causing a clatter. He cursed under his breath, hopping on his good leg and regaining his balance. "That's cheating, Doc."

She grinned, pointing a finger at him. "Not cheating. Proving a point. I know you hurt your knee the night of the attack, but you were walking pretty well earlier today. Now, you're barely able to stay upright and you're shuffling your feet when you walk. Did you re-injure yourself?"

"Nothing that won't heal." He turned away and hobbled to the desk Vivi usually occupied. "Have a seat."

She was still awkward with the crutches, moving slow as he grabbed her suitcase to slide under the desk. "If you didn't re-injure it, that means you're overdoing it. We've made incredible strides at getting you on your feet, but it's okay to admit you need rest."

"Look who's talking," he mumbled. He received a jab in his side in response, and he nearly went down again. "Dammit, woman, would you quit doing that!"

She laughed at his outburst, her hand lifting to stroke his cheek in another unexpected move. "We are quite the pair, aren't we?"

At her touch, he swallowed the sudden longing that rose in his throat. It had been a long, long time since anyone had done that. Looked at him like she was. He tried to speak, found that yearning trapping his words, and cleared his throat. Still, his voice came out rough. "Amelia, I..."

Her finger moved to his lips, silencing him. "Thank you for this."

It left him speechless, the sudden rush of her so close, touching him, thanking him. He was lost in her soulful eyes and instinctively kissed her palm. The smile she gave him made his heart beat like a timpani under his ribs. The sound was so loud in his head, he wondered if she could hear it, too.

"I have one other request," she said softly.

"Name it."

But before she could, his phone rang with the tone reserved for Beatrice.

The moment gone; Amelia smiled ruefully. "You better answer that. I'll poke around on here"—she pointed at the keyboard—"and pull up my planner."

As his cell rang again, she wiggled herself into the chair and touched the keypad.

This time he swore mentally, gritting his teeth as he made his way to his desk. "Yeah," he said into the phone.

"Sorry to interrupt your dinner, but we have a problem." Beatrice didn't wait for him to ask in regards to what. "Ian's plane went down in Ohio. I'm sending you the coordinates. We don't know how many, if any, survivors there are. I need to know who we have on the ground in that area and how fast they can get there to search for him."

"Holy shit." His insides turned to ice. Amelia glanced over as he sank into his chair, everything else put on hold. "Fucking kid better not die on me. I promised Vivi..."

"Get me that info," Beatrice demanded before she cut the connection.

"What is it?" Amelia asked.

"The tadpole went and got himself fucked." His fingers flew over his own keyboard as he checked the coordinates and found they led to a cornfield in the middle of nowhere. He brought up current assignments, the anger in his guts surfacing, if only to hold down his fear.

"Oh no." She hobbled to his desk; crutches left behind. "Please tell me he isn't dead."

He punched in Beatrice's number, cradling the handset between his cheek and shoulder as he accessed Ian's SFI cell and saw the blinking dot. "Wait a minute," he muttered, looking at the two maps.

"Talk to me," Beatrice said.

"His phone is at Dulles. Are you sure he was onboard that plane?"

"What?" He could sense her coming out of her seat. "Did you call it?"

He was already using a second line to do just that.

"Dude," Ian said. "Don't yell at me, okay? I screwed up and missed my flight, but I'm already booked on another that leaves in an hour. And, I have a really good excuse. Remember that dodgy guy I noticed last week when you sent me here to look for spies?"

Every ounce of anxiety flooded out of Rory and into the floor. He flopped back in his chair, making it rock. "You fucking bastard."

"What? It's only a missed flight! Settle down, old man."

Into the other headset, he told Beatrice, "The tadpole

is fine and healthy—at least until he gets back here and I shove his head up his ass. He missed his flight."

"Rory," Ian said, "this is important."

"Thank God," Beatrice breathed in his other ear. "Tell him to call me ASAP. His wife, too." She disconnected.

Rory felt like he'd been on the verge of a heart attack, and the adrenaline made him twitch. Amelia had caught onto the fact that everything was okay and offered a relieved smile as she headed back to her cubicle.

"Check the news, dipshit," he growled at Ian. "Then call your wife and Beatrice."

"Do they really need to know I screwed up on my first training op?"

Fucking kid. "Yes, in fact, they do. Now get your shit together and do what I said. You're damn lucky to be alive."

"Fine, but that guy I flagged last week—I saw him again today. Here, nearly in the same place as last week. Something's fishy. I'm sending you his photo."

Rory rubbed his eyes. "Look, tadpole, maybe he *is* a spy, maybe he's not. Doesn't matter right now. Do what I said. Vivi. Beatrice. Now."

He hung up.

Amelia didn't say anything more and he was grateful. Shit happened on a regular basis with field ops—he was used to it. Thrived on helping SFI operatives get out of scrapes and jams, in fact. But something about this had jarred him.

I am getting old and soft. Worrying about these new recruits...damn it. He was acting like Ian's father rather than a mentor.

"Can I ask what happened?" Amelia watched him from her chair. He could see the digital calendar on her screen. "Everyone is okay, right?"

"We're all good." He massaged his knee, shifted gears. Shoved the fear and anger back into the hole. "How's your schedule looking?"

"Well." She tapped her fingers on the desktop, concentrating. "I should be able to shift tomorrow's sessions to Tuesday and two to Wednesday. That gives me tomorrow and Monday off. The one person missing is"—she glanced over her shoulder at him—"you. From the way you're gimping around, I'm guessing next Saturday is the earliest we'll be able to do any legwork. We can concentrate on your upper body tomorrow at three."

"Amelia, you just got out of the hospital. Hell, you may need physical therapy yourself. No one will die if you take a few extra days off."

She used the touchpad to open a folder, searching for a file she wanted. "The best thing I can do is get back to work."

The damn woman was going to kill him. He took a moment to breathe so he didn't swear at her bullheadedness. *Let it rest.* He would let her think she had the upper hand and keep her where he could have an eye on her. That was still his best move.

Besides, he had five different fires to put out by the looks of what Beatrice was sending him via their internal server. His phone dinged with a text from Ian, and Rory barely gave it a glance as he pulled the plug on the training mission and sent the details about a future date, time, and place to Ryker and Mia. Thank the heavens they hadn't been on that plane.

Down the rabbit hole of SFI he went and a soft rippling bell sound brought him out of it a while later. He kept his eyes on his three screens, checking on information involving the crash, confirming details around a new Rock Star assignment that involved a high-level intelligence agent in trouble with a Mexican cartel, and lining up the staff who would be moving the bulk of their servers to the new headquarters site Thursday.

The rippling bell got closer, louder, and someone cleared their throat. He looked up to find Amelia frowning at him and holding out her phone with the alarm going off. "We are now going on thirty-six minutes. You said every thirty. Whatever you're doing, stop and take a break."

"I wish I could but—"

"Don't give me that. We've been down this road before with you, remember? If I never hauled your butt away from this computer, you would still be in the wheelchair. There's never a good time with you. To quote a wise man, 'No one will die if you take a break.'"

The argument in the back of his throat died at the look she gave him. With a sigh that came all the way up from his toes, he clicked out of two of the programs and left the one with the news to run. There hadn't been any updates about the crash, and from all accounts so far, it sounded like pilot error. "Yes, ma'am." He stood as she shut off the alarm. "What would you like to do?"

"I am stiff and need to clear my head. I thought maybe we could visit the gym so I could do a little stretching and maybe walk the track once. Are you up for that?"

Stretching would work. Walking? Neither of them would get far. "Absolutely, but don't think you're going to overdo it on my watch. At the first sign of dizziness—"

She interrupted him. "I know, I know. You're a broken record, you know that?" Placing an arm around his waist, she walked him toward the door that led to her side of the underground level. "I promise after that I will go to bed. Or I'll sleep on the couch, I mean."

"The hell you will. You're taking the bed."

Together they pushed on the glass door, nearly head-butting each other before she let go and laughed. "And where will you sleep?"

"On the floor." At least to start. Once she was out, he would return to work and catch up on the missions that had been running without him. He'd be sure to check on her frequently, but he wouldn't be able to sleep anyway with her in the room. "Done it plenty of times."

He expected an argument but none came. She leaned into him, keeping her arm around his waist and they found an easy rhythm, using each other for balance. "You're really something, you know that?"

It wasn't the first time someone had said those exact words to him, but coming from her, it sounded...nice. Complimentary, even. "Why is that?"

She allowed him to open the door into the rec area and he ushered her through. "This place would fall apart without you."

The sincerity in her voice gave him pause. He stared at her back as she took a couple hesitant steps without him, looked around at the space she usually occupied, and smiled.

She'd fiddled with her hair while sitting at the desk, and the ends of it hung in soft curls barely past her shoulder blades. She was still wearing her lovely outfit, and it fit her like it was made for her curves. Curves he very much hoped to see without any clothes someday.

Just like that he was spinning out a fantasy about her and him in his room tonight. Another rabbit hole, but this one more dangerous. That smile, her soft laughter, those sexy full lips of hers. He imagined unbuttoning her blouse, slipping that skirt off her hips. Running his hands down her long, long legs, and—

"Rory?"

Snapping out of the daydream, he found her staring at him with a confused look on her face. "Where did you just go? Paradise?"

"Yeah." It was the closest he would ever come to it, anyway. "Something like that."

NINE

Amelia had glimpsed that same expression on Rory's face in the past. She wished she had x-ray vision to see whatever caused it. His face transformed into one that was so handsome it stole her breath. One minute he was grumpy and gruff and the next, he looked like he'd seen an angel.

Trouble was, he was looking at *her*.

No angel here.

She lifted a brow.

He hemmed and hawed before he motioned at their surroundings. Like any gymnasium, it smelled of equipment and sweat, laundered towels and metal. "Never thought I'd say this, but it's good to be here."

With you. The words were left unspoken, but she saw it in his eyes when they shyly met hers.

Rory Tephra. Shy. Maybe she did have brain damage.

That was a one-eighty turnaround from the man she knew. Even with the great strides they'd made to get him walking, he still seemed to avoid this facility and her. Well, maybe not her specifically, but definitely their physical therapy sessions.

She knew how much he hated feeling helpless, or appearing that way, and she'd tried to reassure him that she did not see him in that light. She saw a fallen soldier who'd been through hell and worked his way back to sanity. Saw a man who, in her book, was a hero, like all of those who worked at SFI. "It is, isn't it?"

They stood there smiling at each other for a long moment that became awkward. He cleared his throat and she glanced away. She nudged him and they used each other for leverage as they walked toward her office, passing the basketball court where he liked to play on his good days, and the weight machines currently in use by two former SEALs—Asher Pierce and Tate Landrum.

She and Rory acknowledged the men who were grunting and sweating, and both stopped their reps to inquire after her health. "A stress fracture and a mild concussion," she said, waving it off like it was no big deal.

Tate wiped sweat from his brow with a towel. "Shouldn't you be on crutches? My mom had a fracture once. The doctor told her if she didn't stay off her foot, the break could get worse."

"I have crutches. Trust me, I know what I'm doing."

Said crutches were nowhere in sight, of course, and both men glanced at Rory with knowing looks. His voice got low and growly. "I'm taking care of her. Mind your own business."

Ash pressed his lips together, not quite smothering his grin. "And she couldn't be in better hands."

Fast as lightning, Rory rapped Ash on the side of the head. "Careful or I'll kill you in your sleep, boy."

Amelia had observed that Rory only did that to the guys he liked. Weird, but true. A guy thing, Vivi had assured her.

Ash feigned outrage, laughing at the same time. "Good luck, Doc. Let us know if you need anything."

Rory was still grumbling as they limped away, and Amelia stuck an arm through his. "It's not nice to smack people."

"Don't worry, he'll get me back one of these days."

Her office wasn't as spacious as Beatrice's, but it was a generous size and served her well when needing to speak to patients in private. After flipping on the lights, she pointed at the visitor chairs and then at the wall next to her file cabinet. "Put these over there and grab two mats, will you?"

He did as directed, and after some shuffling about, they were on their backs with their feet resting on the seats of the chairs, staring up at the ceiling.

"Never realized how ugly that is," she said.

"Textured ceilings were all the rage when this place was built."

Silence drifted between them, and Amelia searched for something to talk about that didn't involve the mugging or the plane crash that had upset him so much. She couldn't exactly ask him what he was working on. Most of what he did was classified, even to those who worked here. Truth be told, she didn't really want to know all the stuff.

"I have two tickets to Hannah's fundraiser." At least that was a safe topic. "It's for a great cause, too. I don't suppose you could take a couple hours off Thursday and go with me?"

He went absolutely still and she peeked from the corner of her eye at him. Maybe it was the angle, but she could have sworn there was stark fear on his face.

"I mean," she stammered, "as friends. If that's what you want."

He seemed to force a breath into his lungs before responding. "Big social gatherings, especially those involving the First Family, aren't my thing."

"Okay, sure. I get it." She didn't, though. "You know Hannah doesn't care what you did before you went to work for SFI. She probably doesn't even know who you are."

He backtracked. "No, it's not that. Well, I mean, that's good that she doesn't know, but I was referring to... never mind. It doesn't matter."

She pushed up onto one elbow to peer down at him. "Yes, it does. To me. Tell me why you don't want to go."

His body tensed. The hesitation before he spoke made her think he was choosing his words carefully. "The last one I attended went poorly for me."

"Ohhhhh." She smacked her head with her palm. God, she was an idiot. Of course he didn't like large social gatherings—he'd been shot at one. That much she knew. She reached for his arm, squeezing it. "I forgot. I'm sorry. What was I thinking?"

He shrugged it—and her hand—off. "Eh, no big deal. Don't sweat it."

She flopped onto her back once more. She should just give up the idea of dating. Give up on anything but focusing on her work. At least she was good at that. "I should do some isometric exercises. Join me?"

There was a slight hesitation again, and then whatever he was about to say, he let it go. "Think I'll do some core."

Over the next few minutes, the awkwardness abated as they each concentrated on themselves. Eventually, they moved the mats away from the chairs so they could have more free range, and he spotted her while she did a few lifts with her good leg and a set of easy seated stretches. She kept losing her balance and ending up on her side laughing, drawing a smile from Rory as well.

She fought off a yawn and he got to his feet, offering her a hand. "Time to put you to bed."

The images that conjured made her cheeks heat. She allowed him to help her up, averting her eyes. "Are you joining me?"

Gentle hands took hold of her arms as he turned her to face him. He lifted her chin so their eyes met. "You're safe here, you know."

He thought she was afraid of being alone. She was, but that wasn't what she'd been insinuating. Was he purposely being dense? Did she need to take out a billboard ad?

She swallowed hard, needing to admit to him how she felt, but not knowing exactly how to get the words out. "Logically, yes, I know, but I only actually *feel* that way when you're in the same room as I am."

His hand slide to the side of her head and she allowed herself to relax into it. "I'm not going anywhere, and if your doctors—including Sloan and Montgomery—give you the all-clear for the party, I'll go with you."

That light feeling filled her chest like a balloon inflating. "You will?"

"I will."

It was asking too much. "You don't need to. I understand."

His other palm came up, enclosing her head so gently it stole her breath. His thumbs brushed against her hair, massaged tiny circles around her temples. "It's time for me to get back out in the world, and I hope you know by now that I would do anything for you."

This was her opportunity. Time to make sure he understood her intentions as clearly as she could make them. She grinned. "*Anything?*"

The corners of his eyes narrowed, suspicious. Then he loosed a breath and nodded. "Whatever you want."

She slid her arms around his neck, one hand sliding to the back of his head and drawing his lips down. "Kiss me," she said.

For half a second he froze again, and then he did.

TEN

It all happened so fast. Her lips were soft and warm, the kiss tender. He wanted more, so much more, but right then, he only wanted to savor every precious moment of his mouth on hers.

She made the tiniest noise in the back of her throat and it sent heat straight to his groin. He drew her closer, feeling her lips part and allowing him total access.

The world melted away and he could smell the faint scent of lemon. He breathed in deeply, relishing the fact he could detect her natural sent under it.

Her fingers raked through his hair. He hadn't put it back tonight, leaving it down. She wound a piece in her fingers and pressed her breasts against his chest.

Her tongue teased his and the moment grew hotter. Her lips became more ardent, her hips brushing against him. He rested his hands on them, tucking her even closer and praying this moment of heaven might last forever.

She was shorter than him and she snugged into his

embrace as if she were made for it. Another of those whimpers issued from her as their hips connected, his cock growing hard as steel at the sound, and leaving no doubt as to what he wanted.

No—*needed.*

She rose on tiptoes, tightening her grip and letting him know she wanted him, too.

He lifted her and she wrapped her legs around him, but the injured one kept sliding down his butt and leg. His knee howled with fresh pain, his already stressed legs threatening to buckle. Pivoting, he broke the kiss and swept a hand across her desktop before planting her there.

The books nestled between two bookends, along with a stack of files, crashed to the floor. She didn't seem to care, baring her neck to his mouth and digging her nails into his shoulders.

He trailed kisses over her jawline, nibbled her earlobe, and skimmed her neck. The desk wasn't high enough for an adequate fit between them, but hell if he cared.

And then his fingers brushed across the slim bandage at the base of her skull and he reared back. *What the hell am I doing?*

"Rory?" Her lids were at half mast, her lips swollen from his kisses. "What's wrong?"

Only everything. She'd been through a trauma, was still recovering, and here he was taking advantage of her vulnerability. "Nothing. You're beautiful and I want nothing more than to continue this, but..."

Her finger stroked his brow and she licked her lips. "What?"

A groan started deep in his gut and he had to force it away. "We should take things slow."

"Slow?" The lust in her eyes cleared somewhat. "Is that what you want?"

Hell no. He calmed his erratic breathing, feeling like he'd ran ten miles. What he wanted was to take her right there, and then again in his room. And again and again and again. She deserved better than that. Better than him. "That's what *you* should want. After what you've been through, you may simply be acting out because of the shock and distress of being attacked. It happens. Used to see it all the time in the field. Operatives often get a scare and the first thing they want to do is...well, *feel* alive. Some drink, some jump into risky behavior, and a few find a willing partner and knock boots."

It took a second for her to digest his words. Her face went three shades of red. "You think I want to sleep with you because I was mugged?"

He shrugged, hoping against hope that wasn't the reason. Still... "It happens."

Belligerence distorted her features and she shoved him with a level of strength he hadn't expected. He nearly ended up on the ground. "You asshole!"

He caught himself on the edge of the desk, swinging his upper body around and accidentally brushing her nose with his. *So, so close.* His breath hitched for half a second and then he straightened. "Okay, maybe I deserved that, but it's true." He managed to stand on his two feet and plastered on his best glare as he crossed his arms over his chest. "Ask Vivi. She'll tell you."

"I can't believe this." Sliding off, she wobbled, but

when he reached to steady her, she jerked out of his grip. "I know I suck at flirting, but I've done everything I can to show you that I—"

A knock at the door interrupted and they both glanced in that direction.

Who the fuck?

"What?" Rory barked.

"Everything all right in there?" It was Ash. "We heard a crash. Do you two need help?"

"No we don't fucking need help. We're not invalids!"

Rory felt Amelia's hand cup his shoulder, attempting to pacify his temper. "Thanks for checking on us," she called. "I accidentally knocked some books off my desk is all."

"Okay." There was an awkward, too-long pause, as if the men were debating whether to push or relent, then, "See you later."

When they'd moved off, Rory drew a breath and faced her. "We're both tired and not at our best. Let's take a break, regroup, discuss this tomorrow. Okay?"

Hurt shone in her eyes and there was nothing he could think of to take that away. "It's not okay," she said, heading for the door. "But I'm not wasting my breath."

He caught up to her, taking her arm and placing it around his waist. "You have to keep weight off that foot," he insisted over her protests. "If you don't follow the doctor's orders, I'll report you to Beatrice."

"You wouldn't."

"Try me."

"You *are* an asshole."

It would have smarted if her voice had still held

rancor. "Never claimed I wasn't." He helped her across the threshold and closed the door behind them. "Seven days."

That sparked curiosity. "For what?"

"I want you to give yourself—*us*—seven days. Allow yourself to process what happened. Talk to Vivi, take care of your ankle. If you still want to..." What should he call it? Date? Fuckin' A. "If you want a relationship, I'm all in. We'll start slow and build up. See where it goes."

She was quiet as they imitated snails on their return to the Ops room. The silence felt like razors in his stomach. Would she agree? Tell him to fuck off?

He led her to his quarters, flipping on a light as they entered. "You're the reason I can do this." He eased her into his favorite recliner, glad that it was clear of clothes and dirty dishes. He often ate and slept in it.

She sighed as she sunk into the cushions. Tiredness seemed to weigh every movement. "Do what?"

"Move like this." He gathered a blanket and showed her how to operate the buttons to get the chair to recline, then laid the cover over her. "Get some sleep. I'll check on you in a little while."

She gripped his arm to stop him from leaving. "Rory."

"Want me to bring you some water? Your pain meds?"

"No, I don't need any of that. I agree to the seven day thing, but I want a reward for it."

He placed his hand over her much smaller one. "Anything."

"Go with me to Hannah's fundraiser Thursday night."

He stuttered, cursing himself. "I know it means a lot to you, but you should stay here, out of the limelight."

The corners of her eyes creased as she narrowed them at him. "Why?"

How to explain because his gut said so? "Until we capture your assailant, it would be wise for you to avoid public crowds."

He started to pull away but she held on. "That makes no sense. First of all—"

"I know you don't believe it was anything but a random crime and you think I'm being overly protective, yada, yada, yada. I admit it—I am. You gave me my life back, Amelia, and it's because of me that you were in that alley to begin with. I could have lost you. Could have lost...everything. Again."

She blanched. "But you didn't. I'm right here, and it wasn't your fault."

"You and everyone else can say that until you're three shades of blue, but I invited you out for dinner and that's why you were there. If you really believe the attack was random, then it *is* my fault. You wouldn't have been anywhere near that alley otherwise."

"You didn't cause the accident that backed up traffic, nor did you force me to leave Jose's car and trek through that alley to get to the restaurant. I can't understand why you're being so stubborn about this."

There was so much she didn't know. *Better if she never does.* But something she'd said flipped a switch in his brain. "Get some rest."

He scooted back to Ops and plunked down in his chair, his fingers moving over the keyboard before his ass hit the seat. *You didn't cause the accident.*

What had?

While he was digging for a police report on that, he called Moe. "Did you check traffic cams around the car accident?"

"Sure." He yawned; his voice groggy with sleep. "Jesus, Tephra, it's after midnight."

"Did you notice any vehicles sticking close to Jose's car from the time it left here until it got to the accident?"

In the background, the mattress springs creaked as he sat up. "I was looking for a man in black on foot, not vehicles."

Exactly. "Get your ass down here and help me review footage from around that area. We need to go over it as well as what led up to it. I want to know if Jose and Amelia had a tail."

Another yawn but his voice was more alert. "Be there in five."

Rory disconnected and started reading the accident report.

ELEVEN

Rory braced his hands on each side of the frame, staring down at the knob. The sign on the door read *In Session* and he knew better than to interrupt Vivi and her patient. He shouldn't even stand here, listening to the murmur of their voices.

But he needed help, and he needed it now.

He mentally smacked himself. Since when did the legendary Rory Tephra admit that he needed anything?

Yes, he'd been coming to Vivi now for nearly twelve weeks, and he'd benefited from every one of those sessions.

This was different. This wasn't about blasting through the blocks that kept him in his wheelchair, or learning to mentally focus and gain clarity like he had when he was in the field so he could juggle the current multitude of important jobs on his plate.

This was about emotions. Love and lust and... *The old me still lurking in the shadows.*

Commitment had never been important to him. Not

the romantic kind, anyway. His SEAL team brothers? Absolute dedication. His country? One hundred and ten percent allegiance. He would do anything and everything for those in his circle.

Love and marriage, though—that was a horse he'd never been cut out for. Rory Tephra liked his freedom, loved his independence.

But he wasn't *that* man anymore.

Because of Amelia.

Also because of Beatrice and Vivi. They'd never given up on him, kept pushing him, kept believing in him. All these women in his life were screwing him the fuck up.

He was so in his head that he didn't hear the approach of footsteps. The door opened and *whoops*. Parker stood there.

She frowned and he lurched backwards, thankful he didn't lose his balance. "Sorry," he mumbled. The old Rory would never have apologized, but he respected Parker, and the last thing he wanted her to believe was that he was listening in on her private conversation with the therapist. "I wasn't eavesdropping. I mean, not intentionally. I didn't hear anything, I swear."

"Rory?" Vivi's voice came from behind Parker. It held annoyance but also worry in every syllable. "Is something wrong? Is Amelia okay?"

Was she? He wasn't sure. "It's not about her." Not really. He didn't need a psychologist to tell him this shit was his baggage, not hers.

Parker stepped into the hallway, turning away from him, but not before he noticed her eyes were red. Had she been crying?

Fucking Moe.

He touched her shoulder and she pulled up short, glancing back. "He's a wanker," Rory murmured quietly, using one of Moe's favorite words, "but he loves you. He would do anything for you, including lay down his life to save yours. Keep that in mind when he's being a bastard."

Parker snorted and wiped at the corner of an eye. "Are you playing therapist?"

"The world would be in deep shit if I were," he admitted.

Her chuckle was forced. "Unfortunately, it's not about him."

Roger that. Maybe Parker was doing her own soul-searching these days. He smiled at her in solidarity. It was good to know he wasn't the only one riding the wildest roller coaster he'd ever been on. "I swear on my own grave I wasn't spying on you." He pointed at his temple. "I've got too much of my own shit going on in here at the moment to... Well, you know."

"Don't we all?" Parker patted his arm. "Go on in. We finished anyway."

"If you need anything—"

She smiled. "Normally you would not be the first person I would call, but I do appreciate the offer."

He pretended to be offended, placing a hand over his heart. "I hope I'm at least in the top five."

She raised three fingers. "You're after Trace and Savanah, but only because Trace and I've been through so much together, and well, she's my sister."

He winked at her, watched as she walked away, and then faced the devil glaring at him from behind her desk.

"Close the door," Vivi ordered, motioning him forward. "Take a seat. I assume this is important."

He did, squirming because of what he needed to ask. He gripped the armrests, forcing himself to be still. *I do not squirm under any circumstance,* he reminded himself.

The good doctor removed her reading glasses and tossed them on the desk. "Our session isn't until tomorrow."

He hadn't even remembered. "I froze up."

She didn't miss a beat. "Why?" Her brows furrowed as she put two and two together. "You mean, in bed?"

He blanched. He'd always been so good at hiding things, keeping secrets. "It didn't get that far, and please tell me that not everyone in the whole building realizes she and I were with each other last night."

She pursed her lips, but he could see the smile in her eyes. *Fuck me, they do.* "Maybe you should start at the beginning," she suggested, "and walk me through it."

He tapped a thumb against his leg. At least his knee wasn't swollen today. "After dinner, she had one of those hit-and-run headaches. I think she was starting to remember something and her brain must have slapped the vault shut again. I tried to get her to see Jax and she refused, but agreed to stay with me. I brought her down to Ops, and then the Ian fiasco happened, and I was trying to catch up on my work. After a bit we took a break."

He rubbed a hand over his face, through his hair.

Vivi took out her notepad, put her reading glasses back on, and started writing. "Did she actually remember something from the mugging?"

"No."

"Go on."

"We were in her office and we were doing a few stretches and talking, nothing more, and then she wanted me to kiss her."

Vivi stopped and peered over the top of her glasses at him. "And you couldn't remember how to do that? Didn't want to?"

Jesus, talking about this was going to kill him. He fumbled for the right words. "That's just it, I *did*. A lot. And I wanted to do more, and I think she wanted to as well, but then I started getting all up in my head. Every time I take a step forward, I have to think about my motivations, and there was no script for this. I mean, she went through a huge trauma, she has a concussion, and she's obviously not thinking clearly."

Vivi turned that over and made a note. "Do you really believe that, or are you using that as an excuse to not pursue this? You do have a pattern."

Now she was trying to piss him off. "Let me make this clear, for the hundredth time, I want a relationship with Amelia."

The doctor smiled. "Good to hear you say it." She blew out an exaggerated sigh. "I wasn't sure you were ever going to admit that."

"I didn't realize that was in question. My problem is that I'm not sure she's ready for a relationship with *me*. With all of my baggage."

"That's her decision to make, not yours."

He rubbed his eyes. "She wanted to become intimate and I stopped her. What the hell is wrong with me? Oh right, I'm a decent guy now. I need to be sure that I'm not taking advantage of her. She won't admit it, but she's scared. She's never experienced something like this before."

"You know about her father and the house fire, correct?"

"Of course, but this is different. That was an accident, and while it left her grieving and it certainly changed her life, this was a physical attack against her person. Random mugging or intentional assault, her brain is trying to protect her because she's fucking scared. You get that, right, Dr. Know It All?"

Never offended by his comments, she fiddled with her pen. "And you remember that she was attracted to you and wanted a relationship *before* the mugging. That hasn't changed. Is it possible some of *your* fears are ungrounded?"

"I haven't been in a romantic relationship in a *very* long time. You feel me?"

"Since before the shooting." It was a statement, not a question. "You've divided your life into *before* and *after*. Not unusual, but is this about the emotional issues it's bringing up or the physical ones?"

"Both," he admitted reluctantly.

"I see." She laid down the pen and removed her glasses. "Sex is an important part of life, especially between consenting partners. But, it's not *everything*. There are plenty of healthy relationships that don't include that level of intimacy, and if it's simply ED, Jax can prescribe a medicine for you."

What the ever-loving fuck? Okay, now they were *definitely* into uncomfortable territory. He hadn't ever considered that in his mental scenarios, but now that she'd brought it up he had a whole new bucket of worms to worry about. What if he did have sex and couldn't get it up?

When he didn't say anything, she went on. "You masturbate, don't you?"

"Oh my god. You did not just fucking ask me that."

"It's perfectly healthy behavior, and considering your temporary paralysis, it's not an out-of-line question. You can pleasure yourself and finish off, yes?"

He pushed to his feet. "So not going there."

"I'll take that as confirmation that all your parts are in working condition, and please stop acting like a prude. I can't help you if we can't get to the root of your problem."

He headed for the door. "This was a bad idea."

"If not that, what is it that you came here to talk about, Rory?"

He stopped with his hand on the knob. "You brought up her father dying when she was a kid. What if I'm just... a replacement? Someone she feels safe with. For now. Down the road, she's going to realize that she's way out of my league and ditch me."

"I see we've circled back to your lack of self-worth in order to sabotage your own happiness." When he turned to argue, she continued. "Do you really want to live the rest of your life alone? Do you want to be on your deathbed and realize that you checked out of the best thing that ever happened to you?"

He closed his eyes and leaned his forehead against the door. This again. "Of course not."

She woke up her laptop and used the mouse to click

on a file. "I have a three page list of accomplishments, exploits, and operations you've completed in your service to your country. Do you want me to read them to you? I suspect that's the tip of the iceberg. Doesn't seem like you're risk-averse or you would've never become a SEAL. Certainly not a spy. You've faced down criminals, terrorists, and traitors. You've also faced down your own demons time and time again. Yet, a woman who doesn't weigh more than one-hundred-twenty pounds soaking wet, and who wants to go to bed with you, sends you into flight mode. Why do you think that is?"

Pivoting to brace his back against the wood, he slid to sit on the floor. Dropping his head into his hands, he rested his elbows on his bent knees. "Honestly, I have no clue."

He heard the squeak of her chair, and then she was beside him, stretching out her legs and kicking off her heels. Her shoulder bumped his. "You sure about that?"

Her voice was gentle, kind. They weren't therapist and patient in this moment. They were simply friends.

She nudged him again. "Have you ever been in love before?"

His head snapped up and he pinned her with a glare. "*Love?*"

Her grin was pure evil.

He stammered. "I don't... There's no way... I barely know her."

"The heart wants what the heart wants."

His stomach bottomed out and he shook his head. "*This* is what it feels like? I'm so screwed."

"Yesterday, when I thought Ian might be dead?" She

shuddered. "God, Rory. My whole world crashed down. Everything just stopped."

And here it was again—these women in his life bringing out his need to protect and comfort. Sighing, he put an arm around her shoulders, giving them a gentle squeeze. "But he's fine. He's got good instincts, too. He sent me a photo of a guy he saw that tripped his radar. I ran it through facial recognition software and got a hit."

She pulled back a couple inches to look at him. "And?"

"Airports are like small cities. Criminals seek the weakest targets, and our guy is on Interpol's list for stealing travel documents to conceal his identity and cross borders undetected. He's high up in a human trafficking cartel and he's already being questioned by the FBI and Homeland. Interpol will get a turn at him as soon as they're done."

The corner of her mouth quirked. "Because of Ian."

He unwrapped his arm from around, stood, and helped her up. "He's going to make a damn good spy. I'll see to it. So will Parker and the rest of her division. You can count on that."

"Thank you." She slid her feet back into her shoes. "I know I can't protect him from everything, and I know that he doesn't need me to, but it's damn hard not to grab my bubble wrap and put him in the basement with you."

Rory opened the door, nodding. "Totally understandable, but no way in hell. I've got enough *help* as it is."

She took his gripe for the teasing it was meant to be. "You're leaving?"

"I need to think over what you said."

"Have you scripted it? Becoming intimate?"

He shut the door again, giving her a chastising look. "Jesus, what if she was in the hallway?"

"I would invite her in for a session with us. Seems we need more couples counseling around here."

He shook his head in disbelief, but honestly he wasn't surprised. "No, I haven't." That was sort of a lie—he'd certainly *imagined* about every position and place they could try. "Not exactly."

"You should. That always helps, right?"

He started to leave, paused. "We're talking about scripting a sex scene."

"Why not? Script a whole bunch of them, taking into account that there are dozens of things that could change the trajectory of such an encounter. It will help you feel confident and prepared, which are your hallmarks. And"— she gave him a lascivious wink—"fun, besides."

Like always, she was right. Goddamn woman.

"Let me know how it goes." Another wink.

He narrowed his eyes. "Not gonna happen. In that same vein, let's pretend this conversation never did either."

"You know your secrets are safe with me. This room is like a confessional—nothing goes beyond these walls."

"But these walls have ears and gossipy schoolgirls, in case you haven't realized."

"Families are that way—in each other's business. We'll be at the new compound before you know it. I bet you're looking forward to having that incredible Ops center I saw last week at your fingertips."

A few months ago, it was all he could think about.

He'd obsessed with where the contractors should run the cables, the placement of the servers, the layout of the cubicles, especially his bat cave.

Now, all that paled in comparison to what was happening with his heart. He rubbed at his chest where the damn thing seemed to be triple-timing it. "You're sure? About the love thing?"

"You've truly never been in love before?"

He shrugged. "All I know is that I've never felt like this. Scares the shit out of me."

Smiling, she slapped him on the back. "Yep, that's love."

TWELVE

The next evening, Vivi was knee-deep in paperwork when a knock brought her head up.

Amelia stood on the threshold with a bit more color in her cheeks and was only using one crutch. "What are you doing Thursday night at seven?"

"Um..." Vivi shuffled folders and books, searching for her planner buried underneath. She used the digital version for scheduling patients, but preferred paper for personal matters. "Ah, here it is. Let's see... Well, that's our big moving day, so I may be at the new compound setting things up. Rory will need my help."

Amelia's smile faltered at his name. "I'm sure he'll have plenty of volunteers. Hannah is having a fundraiser for Leading Edge and I have two tickets. It's for a great cause and I want you to go with me."

Two tickets. One for her and one for *Rory*, right?

Do I want to know what he's done now to piss her off?

Unsure of what was going on, she decided it would be

best if she got out of the invite. She scrolled down the digital calendar. "Oh wait, I have a client session that evening at six. I'm afraid I won't be able to."

Total lie, that, but there was no way she was getting in between them. Not more than she already was, anyway.

Amelia's face fell the rest of the way. "Maybe Sabrina can go."

"Are you up for it? There's going to be quite a crowd. The press, the paparazzi, the whole shebang."

Creases formed between her brows and her lips thinned. She straightened. "Of course I am."

"Rory can't go with you?" she fished. "Because of moving day?"

"That man! It has nothing to do with moving. He doesn't want me to attend. He's acting like I'm a fragile porcelain doll who's going to break if someone looks at me the wrong way. I'm sick of it. He doesn't want to go, so he's blaming my injuries as a reason not to."

"That's not true!" Rory's booming voice echoed down the hall and into the office. Amelia whirled as he marched up to her, his cane thumping on the floor. "I spoke to Jax this morning and he said it's too soon. You're not ready. It's not safe."

The two of them squared off and Vivi sat back, wishing she had a bowl of popcorn.

"Not *safe*?" Amelia slammed the end of her crutch on the floor. "Your theories are out of hand. Dr. Sloan may advise caution due to my injuries, but you're the one claiming it's dangerous. Even if I believed that somebody purposely targeted me in the alley, how could I not be safe in a ballroom full of people, many of whom will have their own bodyguards present?"

"I was point-blank shot in a similar situation, so save your self-righteousness."

"Ugh!" From the way she smacked her crutch on the ground again, Vivi worried for Rory's well-being. He was going to be eating that thing before he knew it.

Maybe it's time I intervene.

But this was *waaaay* better than reality TV.

Amelia touched her chest. "This is my life, in case you haven't figured that out yet, you thickheaded SOB. I decide what's risky, and going to that fundraiser means the world to me. I need to get out of here. Go get away from—"

The way she stopped raised red flags and had Vivi filling in the blank. Amelia thought she needed to get away from *him.*

Rory was no dummy and his expression went blank. Purposely so.

Uh oh.

"I'm trying to take care of you," he said through gritted teeth.

"You're smothering me. I can take care of myself."

He reached out to touch her arm and she jerked away. "Amelia," he started.

"Don't *Amelia* me. Go away." She made shooing motions. "I need to talk to Vivi. *Alone.*"

The neutral mask vanished and the pain on his face made Vivi cringe. Poor guy. He gave her a pleading look before he wheeled and marched away. *Thump, thump, thump.*

They listened to his retreat until the noise disappeared. Amelia, still in the doorway, forced a bright smile. "Sure you can't rearrange your schedule?"

Vivi motioned to a chair and got up. "How about a coffee?"

"Sure." Amelia made it to the seat while Vivi turned on her espresso machine. "If you have time."

There was never enough of that, but right now keeping busy and not thinking about what had happened with Ian and that plane was needed. With all her heart, she wanted him to hang around here and be with her. Not twenty-four-seven, but within easy reach. She liked when she saw him in the hallways, texted him to meet her for a clandestine tryst in the middle of the day. Right now, he was at the J. Edgar Hoover Building, helping lock up the case on Beyar Ingstrom, the human trafficker he'd fingered at the airport. That was only one of the man's many aliases. "With Ian gone and a bunch of paperwork that I have put off far too long, I'll be working into the evening. I need the break."

She hit the button to grind the beans—she preferred fresh coffee—and considered how she could help Rory and Amelia. She wasn't technically a couple's counselor, yet it felt like she was doing a lot of that these days.

The machine made comforting whirring noises as it filled the first cup with the delicious smelling brew. Once she had a pair of drinks ready, she handed one to Amelia, who'd laid her crutch beside the chair. Vivi returned to her desk, inhaling deeply as she sat. Nothing beat these small moments of happiness, especially after her time in a black site prison.

"Wow," Amelia said. "This is yummy. A lot better than what we get downstairs."

Vivi, still thinking about how grateful she was to be here rather than that awful, dank cell, touched her hair. The ends hung around her earlobes now and she planned to never cut it again. The Sinead O'Connor look the prison had given her was not her style. "Don't tell or my office will become a coffee shop, but you're welcome to fix yourself a cup anytime."

"Thanks."

"How's the head?"

Amelia fingered the spot where she'd been hit. "The swelling is gone but it's a bit tender."

No mention of her lost memories. The forehead bruise was barely noticeable. "And the ankle?"

"I never realized how hard it would be to stay off my feet. I hate the crutches and forget to use them half the time, but if I don't, Jax will put me on bed rest." She visibly shuddered. "Can you imagine me stuck there for six weeks?"

"No pain?"

She shook her head, her ponytail swinging. "Not much. I haven't needed any of the pain meds for it."

Vivi sipped her drink. "Are you still having headaches?"

"A few." She set her cup on the edge of the desk and scooted forward. "Can I ask you a question?"

"Of course."

"Is it unusual or abnormal for a blow to the head to..."

Vivi waited but she didn't continue. "Are you having other issues? Vertigo? Nausea?"

"No." She fiddled with a sleeve. "It's not that. I've remembered something."

"Oh." Vivi exchanged her coffee for a pen. "That's good news. Did you share it with Beatrice?"

"It's not about the attack. It's about...the night my father died."

"Oh?" This *was* interesting.

Vivi had brought her budgies to the office that morning and Sherlock mocked her, echoing the word as he hopped onto the edge of the desk and studied Amelia. *"Oh? Oh? Ooooh, Ian, you rascal."*

Vivi tried not to blush at the shock on Amelia's face. "Sorry. You were saying?"

"Is that weird? For me to recall something from that night?"

"The brain in general acts in illogical ways at times. For all of our studies and experiments, science can't figure out or explain certain things about the way it functions."

Sherlock went back to his perch behind Vivi's desk and nuzzled Watson. Amelia glanced down at her lap. "I don't even know if it's real. Maybe I'm imagining it."

"Let's work with the assumption you're not. What did you remember?"

Amelia picked up her cup, didn't drink. "The night my father died, there was a man who came to our house. I don't think Dad expected him...the details are fuzzy, but the two of them went to Dad's workshop. From what I remember, Mom hustled my sister and me into our hatchback to get dinner. We didn't eat out much so it seemed like a treat. I thought we were going to pick up pizza and bring it home, but we stopped at a diner. My sister got chicken fingers and I chose a grilled cheese, like always." She shook her head and continued. "Mom said she'd get a burger for Dad, and when we went to leave, I had to remind her that she hadn't ordered one. She blew it off and told me not to worry, she'd make him something when we got home." Her voice dropped a notch. "Our house was in flames when we arrived."

"Did your mother tell the police about the visitor?"

"I don't know. I want to call her and ask, but... I mean, it was ruled an accident. Faulty wiring in the attic above the garage. Should I even bring this up? We were all so traumatized, and it was a lot of years ago."

Vivi made a note. "You're asking because you wonder if this man had something to do with the fire."

Amelia met her eyes. "Working here is making me as paranoid as everyone else. My father was a simple man, and a kind one. I can't imagine he had enemies."

"And yet, you're sitting in that chair with a lot of questions about that night."

"You don't think I'm imagining it?"

"I don't. Your brain may have put the memory in cold storage, but it's back now and it's bugging you. Could your sister confirm it?"

"She was only five, and in her bedroom playing when he showed up. I was..." She squinted, as if sorting through memories. "I was in Dad's chair. I was reading to him as part of a school assignment while he fiddled with a clock Mom wanted fixed."

"Can you describe this man?"

"Tall and lanky. Wearing a grease-stained coat and pants, like a mechanic. Wore a ball cap, so I didn't pay attention to his hair, but he had an ugly scar on his cheek."

Those details were too vivid to be imagined. "Call your mom and tell her you've recalled him coming to the house to talk to your dad that evening. Does she remember him, too? If she asks why you want to know, you don't have to mention anything beyond the fact that you're simply wondering if your concussion is confusing you about the past."

Amelia toyed with the cup. "Sounds believable."

Vivi brought up Amelia's file on her computer, creating a new entry and adding her notes to it. "I also want you to inform Rory regarding this. He has a sketch artist he can contact who will do a drawing of the man's face based on what you remember."

"Why?"

For folks who'd never lived in the world of crime and undercover work, it was hard at times for them to wrap their mind around certain possibilities. Still, she didn't want to come out and tell her it was more than likely the fire was not an accident. Not yet. Amelia needed to figure it out on her own.

"I want you to pursue this in case remembering more about *that* trauma unlocks memories about the recent one. Retention and recall don't always follow obvious pathways. Like I mentioned, the brain makes connections that seem illogical on the surface, but there's always a reason. Don't fight it; allow whatever surfaces to take you where it wants to. Think of it as clearing the cache on a computer. Review what's there and then you can decide what to keep and what to delete. You may discover other memories, some of them seemingly inconsequential, like what you ate at the diner that night. Doesn't matter. Your brain is sifting and sorting and that's a good thing."

"Not to sound weak, but I wish it would all go away. It makes me feel inadequate, powerless."

Vivi saved her work and took a sip. "You're not. Just the opposite, in fact. This is a positive development, Amelia. Give it time."

"But what if...?"

When she didn't finish, Vivi sought to reassure her. Rory was right about this at least—something was scaring Amelia into keeping her memories locked up. "One step at a time. First, if possible, verify that the man exists and was at your house that night. Then we'll go from there."

"If he was responsible—"

"We'll cross that bridge when we get to it. Remember, he may be innocent. I'm sure your mother mentioned his visit to the police and they checked into him. Rory can get a copy of the report."

Amelia stared into her cup. "All roads lead back to him, don't they?"

Vivi worked at keeping the smile off her face. "He's a good man with a lot of valuable skills. Sometimes, I have to mentally list them to myself when he's being a dick, but in general, they far outweigh his hang-ups."

"You don't have to tell me."

As if they'd conjured him out of thin air, he appeared in the open doorway. "If you insist on going Thursday night," he announced without preamble, marching into the room and facing Amelia, "then I'm going with you. Also, I'm bringing backup."

Her mouth dropped open, and Vivi sat back, no longer hiding her smile as Parker, Moe, Beatrice, and Cal crowded into the office.

"Got any more coffee?" Moe asked, heading for the espresso machine.

Vivi pointed a finger at him. "Touch it and you die."

"Touch it and you die," Sherlock mocked.

Moe held up both hands and sidled back to Parker. "Touchy much?"

Rory bent down on one knee, bringing himself eye-to-eye with Amelia. "I'm not trying to smother you. Gatherings like this make me twitchy on my best day, and I haven't had a decent one of those in a while."

Her face softened and she issued a slightly remorseful sigh. "Oh, Rory. I know and I'm sorry. You don't have to attend."

"Yes, I do," he said. "Not just for you."

She glanced up at the group. "So, you're all going?"

Parker smiled. "It's for a good cause."

Amelia wasn't fooled. To Beatrice, she said, "You're joining us in order to keep tabs on me."

Beatrice put an arm through Cal's. "We want to support Hannah *and* you. Win-win."

Cal rolled his eyes. "What she actually means is, we want to keep an eye on him." He pointed at Rory.

Understanding lit Amelia's face, and she laid a hand on Rory's shoulder. "In case you have an episode."

Referring to his PTSD. Vivi saw his jaw tighten. Oh boy. Had he told her about it? That was progress.

Apparently so. He bobbed his head once and stood. "Cal and B were there the night I was shot."

"We know his triggers," Beatrice said gently.

Amelia looked abashed, while Vivi thought they all should get awards for this performance.

"I shouldn't have been so hard on you," Amelia said to him, returning her cup to the desk before reaching for her crutch. Rory instantly scooped it up and handed it to her.

"Just to be clear," Moe said, "I'm going for the appetizers and champagne. If he freaks out in the middle of the things, you blokes are on your own."

Parker elbowed him and Rory reached over to boff him upside the head, but grinning like a maniac, Moe dodged it. "You love me, and you know it, Batman."

"Vivi!" Ian sprinted in, interrupting Rory's retort.

She came to her feet. "What?"

He drew up short at the sight of the others, then weaved his way to her side. "The Justice Department handed down formal charges against Ingstrom. Interpol is next in line. I did it. I nailed that bastard's ass."

"With help from me," Rory added with an air of indignation.

Vivi detested Ingstrom because of what he'd done to many unsuspecting and innocent people, yet she felt a smidge grateful for him since he'd been the reason to keep Ian off his intended flight. She slipped her arms around her husband's neck. "Congrats!"

He hugged, then kissed her. Thoroughly. Right in front of their audience.

She didn't care, laughing into his mouth. When Cal cleared his throat and the two of them broke apart, she whispered in Ian's ear, "Meet me in our spot in ten minutes."

His eyes flashed with lust and he winked before tearing out of her office.

She adjusted her shirt and downed the last of her drink. "Looks like I'm no longer needed here. Amelia, you have homework, I believe, and since Beatrice and Rory are both here, now would be a good time to share what you told me with them." She gathered two of the folders and her laptop. "If you'll all excuse me, I'm going to cook my husband a celebratory meal."

That wasn't all she was going to do for him. The others moved aside as she hauled the birdcage with her and headed for the door. "Lock up when you're done."

THIRTEEN

Amelia thought she might kiss Rory when he agreed to let her go with him to the compound two days later.

She planned to kiss him anyway, but the fact that she was getting out of SFI for a break made her heart sing. If she'd been able to work like usual, it wouldn't have bothered her, but since she was on light duty for another five weeks, she was going crazy.

Rory had been equal parts helpful and annoying. He'd made sure she had plenty of good books, puzzles, and her favorite music. After finishing three novels and whipping through all the crosswords, plus, nailing sixteen levels on her favorite candy game app on her phone, she needed an adventure.

She'd even done several sessions with patients in her therapy room and it had gone great, but Jax and Beatrice insisted she stick to less than two a day, and only for thirty-minute intervals.

HQ had become a prison rather than her home.

To breathe fresh air, to get away from the worried looks of the others—yes, today was her day.

Rory and Beatrice had thought it interesting that she'd remembered the man who'd come to her home before the house fire, and her mother had confirmed that she'd told the police. Their official report did not, however, list him or suggest that the fire was suspicious in any way.

That in itself was suspicious, Rory had claimed, but he'd let it go after Amelia had griped at him about his level of paranoia.

She wasn't fooled—everyone had stopped talking about the mugging, focusing only on how she was feeling—but they hadn't stopped investigating. She'd seen the pointed looks between Rory and Moe, had overheard Beatrice tell Trace to run a background check on Jose as well as a list of other people she'd given him.

Even Parker was in on it. She's made up a new training mission for Ian—he was also attending the fundraiser Thursday night with Vivi as his date. Vivi had suddenly rearranged her schedule and had taken him shopping for a tux.

Amelia wondered if Rory was going to wear one. He'd look good in it.

At the moment, the man in question was squinting at a cable running from one end of the room to the other and speaking into Bluetooth. "This will never work. We can't have these out in the open like this. The electrician was instructed to run them all inside the wall."

A waft of fresh air teased her nose as she sat close to an open window. In the other building, they never opened windows for security reasons. Here, the compound was inside several layers of fencing, both physical and electronic. The whole place had the latest in safety measures, including keeping unwanted eavesdroppers out. "The Bat Cave Bubble" Rory called it. Like a Stealth bomber, the place was nearly undetectable from the air thanks to reflective panels, and was almost entirely off the grid.

Birdsong trickled to her and she smiled. She already loved it here, her new PT digs completed and waiting for her first patient.

Using the scooter Rory had brought with them, she angled it for her new office, pausing a moment in the doorway to admire the modern furniture and glass-topped desk that was all hers. Making her way to the white leather chair, she shifted from the scooter to sit in it, running her fingers over the padded arm rests. It even had a footstool so she could recline and rest between patients or when she was working late.

She used it now to lift her legs and close her eyes as the ergonomic back cushioned her into a reclining position. A soft "ahh" escaped her lips. Imagining working in this environment was a dream come true.

Her breathing evened out and she sunk a bit deeper into the supportive comfort. Sleep beckoned, even though she'd been getting plenty in Rory's quarters these past few nights. Seemed she should stay in her own room, but she couldn't seem to make herself return there. Alone.

Never had seven days seemed so long. *Only four more,* she reminded herself.

"Looks good on you," a deep male voice said.

She peeled her eyes open and sighed languidly. "This place is amazing."

"Told you." He leaned on the doorframe watching her, his eyes pools of intensity that sent shivers up her spine.

She swallowed hard. "I noticed several golf carts around back. Take me on a tour of the grounds?"

He glanced toward Ops, seeming to debate with himself. "Sure. I could use a change of scenery."

She waited on a bench in the lobby until he appeared out front, then he helped her climb onto the tricked-out cart. Each one had been given a name that was painted on the front and rear bumpers. Rory had chosen *Batman*. He'd glued a bobblehead figurine of the famous superhero to the dash.

"You have your own transport?"

He grinned smugly. "Yep, this Batmobile is all mine. Any of the tadpoles touch it and I'll sabotage their underwear."

"Pretty sure I don't want to know what that involves."

Much like a golf course, the compound had paved pathways that could be used for bikes, ATVs, the carts, and for walking and jogging. The vehicles were equipped with a communication device, GPS, and assorted weather-proof receptacles for sports equipment, weapons, and tools.

After he took her past all of the buildings, describing them in detail, he drove to the lake. The late spring day was sunny and warm and Amelia turned her face up to the sky, soaking it in.

What if I'd died that night in the alley? Never to have sunlight on my face like this again?

Similar thoughts had reared their ugly heads more than once and every time she'd shut them down. She refused to focus on negative thinking.

Instead, she turned her attention to the man beside her. As per normal, he was dressed in cargo pants and a T-shirt. This one had a faded Van Halen graphic. The steel gray color matched his eyes in the filtered sunlight. "It's so pretty here. So different than the city. Reminds me of home with this lake and the mountains in the distance."

He stared at her with that look he got sometimes, like she was an angel. "Umm hmm."

The embers of lust he'd ignited earlier glowed warm and flickered into flames. She felt flush and happy. They were alone. Mostly, anyway. The others on-site were setting up offices in the main building. "Are you excited about the move?"

"It's been a long time coming."

"Is that a yes or a no?" she teased.

He glanced away. "I have a lot of good memories in the current place. It's been a sanctuary for me."

No surprise there. "For me, too, especially lately."

His gaze swung to hers, dipping from her eyes down to her lips. The breeze was light, toying with her hair, the birds singing. He wanted to kiss her and she knew it, and wasn't this park-like setting perfect for it?

"You're beautiful, you know that?"

Her heart thudded and she couldn't keep from smiling. "When I'm with you, I feel beautiful. Invincible."

That made him smile, and her heart pounded a whole symphony now. So rare, that smile. It made her want to bust out in song, like some Julie Andrews parody.

They both moved at the same time, their lips crashing together. She laughed and jerked back. His smile grew and he shook his head.

"Four days," she said. "And then you're mine."

He was still grinning as he turned them from the lake. "I'll hold you to that."

She marveled at the solar panel field he showed her, explaining about their power grid. Then they buzzed past Cal and Beatrice's new house—a Craftsman style with a nice yard. Cal had planted two maple trees out front, small now, but in the years to come, they would shade the home and be pretty in the fall when their colors changed.

The main building came into view once more. "You know," Rory said without glancing at her, "we still need to talk to my sketch artist."

She'd avoided it as long as possible, but yes, she knew. The scarred man had been making appearances in her dreams, along with her missing handbag and sneakers. In some, he was stealing them. In others, she was frantically smacking him with the purse as he tried to assault her. Or she was crying over her ruined shoes while he laughed.

She'd attempted to sort out the psychological meanings behind them, but that was probably best left to Vivi. Logically, she knew he wasn't her attacker, yet her subconscious still made him out to be so. Because she hadn't seen her mugger's face, was her mind offering the scarred man's in its place?

"We should do that," she said to Rory with more conviction than she felt. "Set up a time to meet with him."

"I'll see if he can come by HQ tonight."

"Sounds good."

He must have heard the reluctance in her voice and gave her hand a squeeze. "It's not painful, I swear."

She chuckled, her skin tingling from his touch. She wanted to jump him right here on the path. *Four days.* "As long as you're with me, I can handle it. Did you rent a tux for Thursday?"

He cringed and the cart slowed. "Do I have to wear a monkey suit? I have a nice tie and slacks."

"Formal attire, and you're going to look amazing."

He acted disappointed and she pinched his ribs, making him laugh. The cart came to a stop and he pulled her to him, parting her lips with his and kissing her deeply.

She scooted across the seat, welcoming it. To hell with four days. She wanted him here, now.

Everything disappeared—the birds, the trees, the path. All there was, was Rory and his lips. His hands. His solid presence, lighting her up from within.

A ringing came from somewhere far off, a vibration in her right hip. She ignored it.

It came again, and he said against her lips, "Do you need to get that?"

She peered at him through half-lidded eyes. "What?"

"Is that your phone?"

The ring was insistent, accompanied by the buzzing. If it was her mom... She pulled it out and saw it wasn't. "Hannah?" she answered. "Impeccable timing." *Not.* "Rory and I were just talking about the fundraiser. We're excited to attend."

Rolling his eyes, he hit the accelerator and they cruised toward the building.

"I'm so glad," the First Daughter said cheerfully. "I was hoping we could chat in person. Can you meet me at your place, say, in half an hour?"

"Is this about joining the board? I really hate to disappoint you, but I don't feel I have the time for it."

"It's not that. I've had a setback with my wrist. My feet went out from under me this morning and I fell. I don't have time to run to the ER and have it checked. You know they'll want to X-ray it and it will take *hours*."

"You're sure it's not broken?"

"Pretty sure. It's flared up my tendonitis, though. Please. If you'll just have a look it for me? Work your magic on it. I know it's a lot to ask, but with the fundraiser in two days, I can't waste time at the hospital. Plus, the press will divert all the media coverage to me and my lack of grace, rather than the kids. I don't want that to happen."

"I understand. I'll see you in a few minutes."

"You're a lifesaver. Oh, and don't think I'm going to take no for an answer about that board position."

Amelia laughed. "I'll see you in a few minutes."

"What's up?" Rory asked, parking the cart and helping her to the door.

"Hannah hurt her wrist a few weeks ago and she fell this morning and aggravated it. She wants me to check it out, make sure it's nothing serious. It won't take long. I can call Jose and have him drive me home."

"Like hell you will." He was once again gruff Rory. "Connor's setting up the reception area. He can take us."

"He has better things to do, and so do you."

A pointless argument. Rory barked an order at

Connor the minute they were inside and before she knew it, she was seated in Beatrice's favorite SUV heading for her home.

FOURTEEN

Rory texted Parker on the way to Amelia's. *What's the latest on Hannah?*

Her response came back thirty seconds later. *Clean. No reason to have anyone attack our favorite physical therapist.*

That was good news, but he still felt uneasy about this meeting. The one good thing about it was that he could size her up in person. The short few minutes he had at the hospital with her and Jose had told him little, except that she seemed genuinely concerned about Amelia's health and happiness.

Another message came from B. *The pipe yielded no fingerprints. Wiped clean.*

Could be our weapon???

Odds are yes.

Didn't help if they had no prints, though.

"Everything all right?" Amelia asked. "You're not having second thoughts about going to my place, right?"

"It's all good." He gave her knee a squeeze. He could control this visit, which was far better than attending that fundraiser. And she was right—he needed to let her spread her wings. The image of Vivi wanting to protect Ian with bubble wrap came to mind, and while he'd love to do the same with Amelia, it wasn't practical.

Being in a relationship with her meant he would have to allow her to do things the way she wanted, not the way he did.

"Why don't I believe you? You look like you're going to your death. Or is this about those texts you're getting?"

Busted. "Chatting with Beatrice, trying to catch up on a few things. Figured the ride over was a good time to follow up with her on our open cases."

Her relief was evident. "I'm not exactly the best housekeeper, so don't be shocked at the mess."

"You, messy? I'm surprised. Your desk is immaculate and you're always so on top of things. Hell, even your files are color-coded."

She laughed, and the sound filled him with joy. "That's work. This is home. I don't need to be organized and I'm only there in the evenings. Like you, most of my time is spent at SFI."

Nodding, he sent off another text, his mind working overtime. This one was to the detective working her case. *Did you follow up on that sedan?*

He and Moe had tagged three vehicles that had been on the same route as Jose's from the moment it had left SFI headquarters and arrived at the accident's nexus. Registration for two of them was easy to run down since the traffic cams had caught their plates. The third was a ten-year-old black sedan whose plates were unreadable. It hadn't strictly tailed Jose, only showing up twice at different intersections, but the mere fact it was so nondescript and had no identifying marks—how often was a car that old spotless?—had raised warning flags with Rory.

"You're really behind on work, aren't you?" Amelia worried her fingers in her lap. "I'm taking up all your time."

"It's not you." Rory waited, but the detective was silent. Either he was ignoring Rory or too busy to reply. Maybe both. "It's the move. We'd planned to phase things from one location to the other over several days but now it looks like we need to postpone it for a few weeks."

"You've been planning this for months."

He pocketed the phone in order to give his hands something to do so he didn't reach for her to smooth out the creases between her brows with a kiss, but...nope. *Hands to yourself.* Four days. He would wait that long.

When day seven hit, though? *Look out.* "Years, actually. Another week won't hurt." It kind of did. He was so ready to be in the new compound at his command center.

Traffic grew increasingly thick, the late afternoon streets filling with workers returning home after their shift and an equal number heading in. "I'm taking an alternate route," Connor called, turning at the stoplight. "Get us out of the worst of this snarl."

Rory's phone vibrated against his chest and he tugged it out. Not the detective, but Beatrice. *Sit rep,* she demanded. *Where is my car?*

Sorry, boss. Needed a lift to Amelia's place. Meeting with Shaker.

Shaker was the codename the Secret Service had christened the First Daughter.

A pause. *Why?*

A sprained wrist from the sounds of it. He debated reassuring her he was in bodyguard mode and Amelia was safe, but his normal knee-jerk reaction wasn't necessary. Beatrice of all people knew it. *Might be good for A to go home, even if only for a bit.*

Now he sounded like Vivi, but it was true. Touching base with familiar surroundings might help Amelia's recall.

Thankfully, Parker had cleared Hannah. The president's daughter would be surrounded by her own top-level security guards. What could go wrong?

Hold the bus, he reminded himself before his paranoia kicked in. Even so, he followed up with: *I smell anything out of place and we're out of there.*

A thumbs up was his boss' reply. That meant the Queen B was comfortable with this. He should be, too.

Amelia brushed his arm to get his attention. "You sure you're okay?"

He realized he was gripping his cell so tight his knuckles were white. "Absolutely." Tucking the device away, he took her hand and tried to make general conversation, ignoring the pounding in his head. "How long have you lived there?"

He knew, of course, but needed to find a topic of conversation that didn't agitate either one of them.

"About four years."

"I'm sure D.C. is nothing like South Carolina."

She snickered. "You've got that right. I like both,

though. The city is alive with energy, and my hometown was quiet and peaceful."

He'd always been a city guy. "I'm not sure I'd know what to do with peace and quiet," he admitted.

"Have you ever wanted a family?" She froze for a heartbeat, her fingers fiddling nervously with her sleeve. "I mean, I was thinking about my childhood, growing up where I could play outside. And Sloane. At the compound, she'll have a whole playground to herself. So much better than the city, in my opinion. Got me thinking about kids is all."

Family. It was a sucker punch straight to his gut. He worked at making his voice sound normal. "At one time, sure. Thought I could have it all, you know? Now?" He shrugged, the hollow ache in his chest dredging up old memories he wished would stay buried. How many times after he was paralyzed did he lose it, yearning for someone to love him, be by his side through that awful time? How many times did he nearly toss his guts at the realization he never would. No wife to love him. No kids to teach basketball or help with their math homework? "Better that I didn't have a wife and kids. I only would have fucked them up."

Her brow furrowed. "You don't seriously believe that."

There was no point arguing. "You want kids, I take it?"

She blew a raspberry. "My sister has two and I love being an aunt, but I don't know. Like you, I'm devoted to my work. Beatrice is quite an inspiration. If she can do it, maybe I can, too."

Her smile was uncertain and for a split second, he wondered what their child might look like if they had one.

"Sloane's going to need friends to play with at the compound."

The smile became sly, impish. "That she is."

They arrived and found the First Daughter and her minions waiting.

Upstairs in the apartment, Amelia apologized profusely for the mess, and Rory found himself helping her collect scattered clothes, move stacks of magazines, and create a space for Hannah to sit.

"Please don't go to any trouble," she said, ignoring the now empty couch and heading for the kitchen. "Really, I know this is inconvenient."

Amelia motioned her to a chair, glancing around as if seeing her place with fresh eyes. "How about tea? I'm dying for some Earl Gray."

"That would be lovely."

Rory made himself useful, fetching cups for them while Amelia filled a kettle with water. He did his best to act casual, pretending to ignore the security agents nosing around. Once they'd cleared the apartment, the lead agent, Masden, gave Hannah a terse nod of assurance, and they removed themselves to the outside.

"You sure you don't want any?" Amelia asked him.

He shook his head. "I'm a coffee guy."

"I have that, too."

He caught her hand before she could start the coffee maker. "I'm good. Take care of your friend."

Amelia dropped a kiss on his cheek, then sat at the table. "Let me see that wrist," she said, reaching for Hannah's hand.

The woman appeared embarrassed when she

explained what had happened. "I was in a hurry, dropped my keys, and well...I ended up rounding a corner too quickly with my arms full of handouts for Thursday night and fell down the steps."

"Did you hurt anything else?"

She grimaced as Amelia unwrapped the ACE bandage to reveal a swollen and bruised area on the outside of the wrist bone. "My pride. They were giving a tour to some school kids and I provided quite a show." The grimace grew as she showed Amelia how she could move her hand in a circle. "I can do this, so I don't believe it's broken, but turning a door handle, or picking up a cup"—she motioned at the two on the counter holding teabags—is impossible."

Amelia gently prodded the swollen skin with her fingers, then gently ran her thumb up the forearm. "Appears to be a strain, but you've fired up your tendinitis. It needs rest, ice, and some anti-inflammatories."

The kettle whistled, and Rory made work of pouring the water. He set the cups in front of them, and Amelia motioned to the fridge. "There's not much in there, but you might find a soda."

Under the guise of searching for a beverage, he listened to them discuss the upcoming fundraiser while Amelia retrieved an ice bag, over-the-counter medicine, and a brace she had on hand.

"How is your mom?" she asked.

"Much better, but so disappointed she's going to miss the event. I'm having Kenesha livestream parts of it just so she doesn't feel totally left out."

While the two women continued to discuss the

fundraiser, he found an orange drink, and having had his fill already of the upcoming event, wandered into the living room to scan Amelia's shelves of assorted books and movies.

Her eclectic tastes made him smile, and he made note of the fact she had a serious interest in reggae. He'd never been good at gift-giving, and rarely had anyone to give to, but now there would be birthdays, Christmases, Valentine's Days. That thought made him a bit squeamish. Was he really thinking that far down the road?

He sure as fuck was.

He glanced through the kitchen doorway, listening to the friends talk and laugh. Deciding to explore the rest of the space, he sipped his drink. Not to be nosy, but to get to know this other side of Amelia better. Her sexy laughter eased something between his shoulders, while it also fired up certain parts below his belt. He caught the scent of lilacs and vanilla, and followed where his nose led.

It had grown dark outside, and no light penetrated her bedroom. He'd been in such a hurry to throw the random piles of clothes and magazines in here, he hadn't taken time to study it. Step by slow, steady step, he paused on the threshold. He didn't intend to snoop, but simply wanted to soak it in.

Funny, he picked up a whiff of fresh air—at least as much as the city allowed. Flipping on the light, he noticed the edge of the curtain moving ever so slightly due to a breeze.

He crossed the room, and sure enough, found the window cracked. Instantly, he went on alert. Pulling out his phone, he texted Trace, asking if he'd noticed it during his search.

Trace responded almost immediately. *Negative. I made sure all windows and doors were locked tight.*

All his training and past experiences snapped his spine straight. He started to rush back to Amelia, then stopped himself. The Secret Service had just checked the entire apartment. There was no one hiding in the closet, or under the bed, ready to jump out and hurt her. Maybe he'd missed it in the rush to clean up the front rooms, and she had cracked it open herself to let some air in.

He had to get over this paranoia and look for other options before jumping to conclusions.

Returning to the kitchen, he apologized for the interruption and pulled Amelia aside.

He thought he looked casual and confident, but she immediately frowned. "What's wrong?"

"Nothing, but I wanted to ask, did you open the window in your bedroom when we came in?"

The frown grew. "No, why?" Her face instantly paled. "Are you saying someone broke in? I thought Beatrice had people watching the place."

Initially, she had. When they couldn't figure out a motive for the attack, nor find a solid suspect, she'd had to pull Trace and the others for different projects, including prepping for the move. Amelia was in no danger since she was at headquarters, and Beatrice had no intention of allowing her to return permanently to her apartment until they'd resolved the situation. Either they declared it a mugging, or found the culprit and made sure he was brought to justice.

Rory groped for other reasons. "Did your parents come by before they left?"

The frown disappeared and her shoulders relaxed. "Oh, my god. Was there food in the fridge?"

"Bagels, sliced cheese, some apples..."

She palmed her forehead. The bruise there had faded to a pale yellow. "That's my mom for you. I chased her off, and she knew I was going to be living at SFI for a while, but she still brought snacks and dropped them off."

He felt his own shoulders ease. "So she might have cracked open the window."

"I don't know why she would do that without mentioning it. I mean, the temperature is mild right now, and she does love to air things out when the weather is nice, but one good rainstorm and I'd need new carpeting. Don't think the landlord would appreciate that."

The landlord. Rory stilled. "Would he ever enter your apartment and not notify you?" It was illegal, sure, but plenty of them did.

"*She*," Amelia corrected, "would never dream of it."

She hobbled to the bedroom, Rory on her heels. At the window, she reached to close it and he stopped her. "If someone's been in here, they may have left prints. Let me grab Connor's kit and dust it."

"Connor carries a fingerprint kit?"

"Doesn't everyone?"

His attempt at humor fell flat.

"Amelia?" Hannah called.

She gave Rory an exasperated look. "Fine, dust it for prints." Then she turned toward the door. "Coming," she called.

On silent feet, he followed her out, scanning every nook and corner as he went and reassuring himself there was no one inside except the three of them.

Downstairs, he motioned at Connor to roll down his window as he approached. "I need the fingerprint kit."

Connor was instantly on alert. "Why?"

"Probably nothing, but I want to dust the bedroom window."

As Connor dug into the set of equipment, stored inside the rear compartment, Rory scanned the street, including the buildings nearby. Nothing seemed out of place.

"Need help?" the kid asked, handing over the black plastic box.

"Nah. I can handle it."

Climbing the outside stairs, he ignored the twinge in his lower back. He slowed his steps, not because of that, but because his headcount came up one Secret Service Agent short.

At the door, the two standing on either side stopped him.

"We need to check that," the agent on the left said. The guy had a buzz cut, a square jaw, and eyes that missed nothing.

His partner continued to monitor the scene behind tinted sunglasses. The third came striding from around the corner of the building.

"All quiet back there." He walked with purpose, adjusting his jacket as he jogged up the stairs, effectively pinning Rory in between the three of them. "What do we have here?"

Rory relinquished the kit without a word, but handed it to him rather than buzz cut. He remembered this guy from the hospital. Flat eyes and not a single laugh line in his face. His suit barely hid his muscled biceps, and as he took it, he locked eyes with Rory for a long moment.

Meant to unnerve him?

Rory stifled his snort as well as his middle finger.

The agent opened the box, rifling through the fiber-glass brushes, dusting powder, and lifting tape. He then checked the case for hidden compartments.

"It's just a fingerprint kit," Rory told him.

The man didn't bother to fix the disturbed tools, snapping it shut and shoving it back at him. "For what?"

"Lifting prints." *Duh.*

"Of the First Daughter?"

"Can't get anything past you. My evil plan is to steal Hannah's identity and use her prints to take over the world." He added a maniacal grin.

The agent's eyes narrowed. "This time try the truth."

Carefully, Rory used the case handle to accept it and put on his most placating expression. He'd dealt with plenty of security details before, and while he didn't blame these three for being ultra-suspicious, he was tiring of this game. "Dude, you know who I am and who I work for. You also know that my girlfriend upstairs was attacked the other night. Today is the first time I've heard her laugh in a week and it's because of Hannah. I'm giving them some time for girl talk and I'm making myself appear useful while they're at it. Cut me some slack. I'm not lifting Hannah's prints to use on biometric scanners. I'm just checking a window to see who might have opened it. Probably Amelia's mother. That's all."

"I'll need to accompany you."

Great. "It's a party, then, but I suspect your dull presence will put a damper on things."

The man motioned for him to lead the way and Rory kept his impatient eyeroll to himself.

FIFTEEN

Amelia heard the door open, saw Rory and Agent Masden enter. Masden took up a position outside the kitchen door and Rory disappeared, heading for her bedroom.

Didn't it figure that the first time she'd brought him home, it wasn't for a romantic evening?

"That's him, right?" Hannah whispered, jutting her chin in Rory's direction. "The guy you were excited about?"

Amelia couldn't keep the smile off her face. "That's the one."

"He looks like a lumberjack."

She scrunched up her nose. "He does not."

"Big, burly, that beard..." Hannah winked. "He doesn't seem your type."

They'd known each other for so long that she couldn't lie because Hannah would call her on it. "I know, but I really like him."

Hannah chuckled. "I can see that." She used her good hand to sip tea. "What did you think of the photos? Did you have a chance to look at them?"

"What photos?"

Hannah pulled a face. "Oh, right. You don't remember anything about that day." She shook her head. "Sorry, I forgot. At my session, I gave you a USB with photos from my mom. I hooked her up with Kenesha Wallace, the teen from Detroit who transfers physical photos and old videos to digital ones and creates these beautiful scrapbooks from them? Remember me talking about her?"

That *did* ring a bell. Amelia felt a touch relieved. "Your mother has as many pictures as she does recipes."

Hannah laughed. It was a running joke that the First Lady considered herself quite the chef but never actually cooked. That didn't stop her from collecting recipes from her travels, as well as thousands of photos and videos of the family on the various campaign trails and precious few vacations. "I've tried to Marie Kondo her, but it isn't working. Kenesha is slowly but surely going through all of our family pictures and recordings and organizing them. She does great work and I anticipate she's going to get lots of press over this. Mom's been singing her praises on social media."

Amelia's tea was tepid now, but the mint flavor soothed her. "And you gave photos to me? Why?"

"Copies of shots from a fundraiser near your hometown years ago. I was eight, so you were, too. Some major investors set up a bird sanctuary outside of town and my parents were on the campaign trail—when weren't they? Your dad was there. Did you know he was into birds?"

Amelia set the cup down a bit too hard, the clang setting her teeth on edge. "My dad? Nah."

"I'm pretty sure it's him." She pointed to the photo on Amelia's fridge trapped by a magnet. "His hair is longer than it was there and he's wearing a nice suit, but I'm pretty sure that's the same guy."

Amelia blinked. "He wasn't a bird watcher."

"Apparently it was a big deal because the mayor at that time, C. Ray Jones, ran a huge logging company that was accused of endangering Bluebirds. There was a lot of mass clear cutting in your state. One of Dad's stops canceled, Charleston I think Mom said, and since he was pushing his environmental agenda and they weren't due at the next one until the following day, his campaign manager thought an event to raise money and awareness about the birds was a great photo op." She finished her tea and rubbed her sore arm. "I'm not sure it's him, but I thought you'd want to see the pictures. I know you don't have a lot of him."

Was it true? Had her father been there and been caught on camera? "That's wonderful. I can't wait to look at them, but... I don't know what I did with it."

"Crud! It was in your Binni bag." Hannah smacked her forehead. "I'll have Kenesha make another copy for you."

Something clicked in Amelia's brain and a searing pain cut from temple to temple. She sucked in a breath and closed her eyes, opening them again when Hannah grabbed her hand.

"Hey, are you all right?"

Flashes of memories slammed into her. "Sure," she lied, reeling. "Just tired."

Hannah stood. "You've overdone it and it's my fault. I better get out of your hair. Thank you so much for the tea and taking a look at my wrist. I owe you."

Amelia pasted on a smile and walked her to the door, barely noticing that Agent Masden hung back. Her chest felt tight and she couldn't decide whether to rub it or her head. "Remember to take care of it," she reminded Hannah.

"See you tomorrow night," her friend called as she headed for the exit. "Get some rest."

Where is Masden? Amelia turned, expecting him to be right behind her. She found him in the kitchen wiping down the table and cup with a dishtowel. "What are you doing?"

He pocketed the cloth and marched past her without giving an answer.

"Hey, that's mine," she yelled. He kept going, the door closing behind him with a firm bang.

"Weird," she muttered.

Trudging to her bedroom, she found Rory lifting tape from the windowsill.

"Well?" She sank onto the bed. If only she could take a nap. "Any luck?"

He held up the tape, with its traces of black powder, near her bedside lamp, examining it. "No."

She sat straighter, eyeballing the lack of swirls on the tape. "No prints?"

"Not a one." He let out an exasperated grunt. "Someone wiped it. Just like the pipe."

Beatrice had told her about the suspected weapon found in the dumpster. Her stomach clenched. "Masden just wiped down the table and cup," she murmured.

"He did *what?*"

She nodded but the movement cost her, and she rubbed her temples. "It's a security procedure, right? Because of who she is?"

He stewed for a moment. "Maybe."

From what she'd observed, there were no maybes in Rory's world. She wondered what that meant. Rubbing the back of her neck, she went to her walk-in closet—one of the few perks of the apartment—and turned on the overhead light. "There you are," she said, reaching for her purse.

Rory appeared in the doorway. "Who?"

She held it up for him to see. "I have two of the exact same Binni bags in this design—one for special occasions, the other for every day. This one is the latter. See how it's worn around the edges and there's a pen mark inside right here?" He nodded as she pointed, but confusion knit his brows. *Right, not important.* "Anyway, since I was running late that night after Hannah's session, I didn't have time to transfer more than my wallet and phone into the special occasions version. That's the one that was stolen, and this one..." She dug through the sunglasses, tissues, miscellaneous change, and other debris collected and never cleaned out. No USB. *Hmm.* She frowned, her pulse tripping over itself as she checked an interior pocket. Her fingers snagged on a tiny plastic case. Bingo. A grin lit her face as she held it up. The cover was in the shape of a cat head. Her friend loved felines. "This one has a USB from Hannah containing pictures of my father."

Rory still looked confused. "Why did Hannah have pictures of your dad?"

"Long story and I didn't remember her giving me this, thanks to my amnesia." She handed it to him. "Sounds crazy, but could it be what the mugger was after?"

He took the tiny drive, eyeing it with calculation. "Who knew she gave this to you?"

Amelia shrugged. "No clue. Her mom. Kenesha, the gal who created it?"

"We need to look at the photos and I need to investigate your friend and her bodyguards in more depth."

Amelia grimaced. "Hannah didn't have anything to do with what happened."

"Come on," he said, "let's get to SFI. On the way, you can tell me the long story about why she has these photos."

SIXTEEN

Rory sat at his desk, scanning through the pictures. Lots of folks in dress clothes drinking too much and mostly smiling in posed shots. Each had at least one of the now-presidential family in it. They'd all been twenty years younger, dreams of the White House in the future.

The young Hannah wore a pink, ruffled dress and looked bored out of her mind in the few she appeared in. She was front and center in one with a group of kids lined up in rows around her. They each held a stuffed Bluebird except for Hannah and a blond-headed boy next to her.

He flipped to the next picture, recognizing several of those surrounding the president and his wife, including Frank Downey, the president's current chief of staff. None of the then-governor's security detail were familiar, though, and certainly weren't the agents now assigned to Hannah.

He'd already put Moe on the job of gathering a thorough background report of each of her current ones, wanting to make sure none had ties to Amelia and her family.

"There," she said, nearly jumping out of her seat. She pointed to the screen at the photo he'd paused on that showed Jacob Clemson and another man with their heads together at the back of the room. "Next to that pillar. That's him! Oh my God, *Daddy!*"

She stroked a finger in the air over his face, then brought her fist to her mouth, a tiny sob escaping her lips.

Rory studied the man in profile as he enlarged the shot. Approximately five-ten or so with short black hair and a stiff stance, her father was dressed in a navy blue suit and was watching Clemson and his companion, his face unscrupulous.

"All of our photo albums went up in the fire," Amelia said quietly. "Mom only had a few pictures of him on her phone. It's so good to see him. Wonder why he was there?"

Rory zoomed out and refocused on the man speaking to the president. "Any chance you recognize this guy?"

She shook her head. "Should I?"

"Just checking. I don't either." He switched to the next and together they scanned it thoroughly. Amelia picked out her father again, and this time he was speaking to the unknown man. Rory checked the metadata on the picture —it had been taken after the man's conversation with Clemson. "I'll run his face through our databases and see if we can get an identity on him."

Over the next few minutes they went through all the pictures, along with a video of Jacob Clemson speaking to the crowd, his wife, Lori smiling beside him.

In that, Amelia's father bobbed in and out of view among the gathered spectators. *What or who is he looking for?*

He certainly wasn't paying attention to the speech and appeared to be there alone, no sight of Amelia's mother or anyone else Amelia recognized as friends or neighbors.

A tickling started between Rory's shoulder blades. He wished he could put his finger on what was causing it. "Let's go through these again, and this time I want you to focus on the other folks, not your father."

"Who am I looking for?"

The tickling amped up. They were onto something, and it was big. "Possibly your attacker."

"What?" She gave a chuckle as if he were joking, then sobered at his expression. "You're kidding." When he didn't nod or confirm it, she became even more solemn. "Rory, I didn't see my attacker the other night, so even if he is in one of these, how would I recognize him?"

He swiveled around, taking her hands in his as they faced each other. Their knees bumped, and she seemed anxious, as if she wanted to pull away but didn't. "How do you know you didn't see him?"

He and Vivi had both asked her the same question when she kept denying she might be able to identify her mugger to the police. "If I *had* seen him, and I could remember what happened..."

"It's normal to be scared to recall his face. Just like being scared of remembering the man who came to your house the night of the fire. But I need you to try. Even if you didn't see him there may be something that surfaces that might lead us to him."

Instead of jerking away like he had anticipated she would, she exhaled slowly and groaned.

That sound, along with the determined look she gave him, sent certain parts of his anatomy into overdrive. He had to snap himself out of it. Every damn thing she did fired up his libido. Simply holding her hands and not being able to tug her close for reassurance, not to mention the other things he wanted to do to her, was driving him nuts. "I'm not scared to remember," she insisted. "I can do this."

"Yes, you can. It helps to close your eyes. Take yourself back to that night in the alley. I'm right here with you, and nothing and no one can hurt you in this moment."

She did as instructed, allowing her lids to shut, but she couldn't *not* complain. "We've already tried this, remember? I'm not good at visualizing. It doesn't..."

Her sudden silence and the grimace on her face suggested the opposite. "What is it?" he coaxed.

Body growing tense, she swallowed, but then gave a weak smile. "Nothing. I remembered I haven't done laundry today."

He chuckled and swore softly under his breath. This woman. He squeezed her hands. "That's what you're grimacing about?"

"No, dummy. My head hurts. Every time I try to recall that night, I get a sharp pain that radiates from the back of my skull to the spot behind my eyes."

He hated to push her, but he needed her to get past that limitation, that barrier. He thought about the times Vivi had brought him to his edge, and, no surprise, pushing never worked. It was a failing of his, maybe, but he always pushed back.

Instead, she'd switched tactics and taught him to relax about the demons chaining him to the past. To imagine the barriers dissolving. He didn't need to bulldoze through every wall in order to access his deepest fears and overcome them. He needed to simply acknowledge and question why they were there. Respect them, and then respect that he didn't need them holding him back anymore.

"Stop and take a deep breath," he told her, doing his best to channel Vivi. After she did so, he continued. "Instead of imagining yourself in the alley, go back to when you were safe in Jose's car. What are you feeling?"

"Excited. Happy. A little anxious."

The last surprised him. "Anxious? Why?"

"Because of you." She peeked open an eye. "You can be very intimidating at times and I really wanted everything to be perfect that night."

He smiled, considering the fact that he'd felt the same way. Damn Vivi for always being right. "What made you want to get out and walk?"

She opened the other eye and stared directly into his. "I couldn't wait to see you."

It took his breath away, that admission. Her look of total honesty. "I was sitting in the restaurant anxious as all hell to see you, too."

"You were?"

"Of course I was."

Her grin turned conspiratory. He returned it.

"I'm not sure I can make it four more days," she whispered.

Another admission he hadn't expected, but damn, he was glad to hear it. "Me neither."

"How about a caveat? If I can remember something right now, our original agreement can be rewritten."

How could he pass up that kind of deal? "You're on."

Motivated and all business once more, she closed her eyes, inhaled, and spoke. "I'm getting out of the car and admiring my flashy pink sneakers. I know it sounds frivolous, but I love those shoes. I hear sirens, and the various noises of the cars due to the traffic jam. I leave them behind and hurry along the sidewalk, following my app with the green line that zigzags through the blocks to get to the back of the restaurant and...yuck, the alley smells terrible." She screwed up her nose. "There are puddles of grossness everywhere, and I hop over one, trying not to ruin my shoes. I'm texting you that I'm nearly there when" —she sucked in a breath, body going rigid.

He held tight when she jerked, trying to pull away. "Breathe and rewind. Stay in your happy place for a minute and allow your brain to dissolve whatever is keeping that door shut on your memories. You aren't there, you're here with me."

Her chest heaved, but the stiffness lessened and she tilted her head as though seeing something behind her lids. "I don't remember being struck. It's fuzzy, but I do recall being on the ground. I heard...footsteps."

"What kind? Light, heavy? Fast, slow?"

"Heavy, methodical. He picked up my bag and took off."

Rory's adrenaline spiked. "Did you see his feet? His hands? Anything before he ran?"

Her eyes narrowed at the corners. "That's the thing, he *didn't* run. He walked. Bold, confident."

Fuck. The mere thought of it made Rory want to punch someone. When he caught this asshole... "You're sure it was a man? What makes you believe so?"

Her eyes opened. "I just know it. He had a confident gait. I've been around all of you so much that I automatically registered it."

"Us?"

"Yeah, you know, men like you and the others here. You have a distinct confidence about you. Like I said, he was bold. As if he did this sort of thing daily." When it truly dawned on her what she'd said, her eyes widened. "Is he military?"

Rory gritted his teeth, the profile of the man becoming clearer. The faces of Hannah's agents flashed across his mind. "You don't remember hearing his footsteps before he hit you?"

She shook her head. "No, but I was distracted."

Or he was as stealthy as Rory initially suspected. Someone with training under their belt and cocky enough to believe he wouldn't get caught.

I've been that guy.

And now someone like him had gone after Amelia. It didn't exactly narrow down their field of suspects, but she was remembering, and that was good. Her attacker had to have been close to follow her the moment she left the car. "Did you pass anyone before you entered the alley? Notice anyone watching you? Did anyone stand out? Make you feel uncomfortable?"

Her eyes lit. "I passed a bunch of people. There were

lots of gawkers at the scene of the accident when I passed by. I remember!"

"You didn't recognize any of them?"

"I wasn't paying attention. I was in a hurry and texting you."

He released her hands with a squeeze and patted her knee. "You're making great progress."

"Is it enough, though?"

"I'll check the street cameras and pull stills for you to look over."

"Now? Tonight?"

Strain warred on her face against pleasing him. He brushed a finger over her jawline, down her neck, aching to trail kisses there.

She sighed and some of the turmoil left her features. Her head shifted to rest her cheek in his palm. Desire flickered in her eyes.

And hell on a stick, his entire body went into overdrive. Clearing his throat, he faced his center screen again and brought up the first photo. "Let's start at the beginning. Look at the other people in the crowd, the decorations, the food, all of it. Put yourself there and see it from your Dad's eyes. Why was he there? Who was he talking to? Why them?"

"Wait just a minute." She grabbed the arm of his chair and forced him to face her again. "We had a deal."

He couldn't keep the eager grin off his face. "Guess I have to pay up now, don't I? After we do this, okay?"

She jumped into his lap and he laughed as his chair rocked backwards, but all thoughts of falling over or keeping her focused on their mission fled when her mouth touched his. As if desperate, she sunk her hands into his hair, pulling him closer, her lips on fire.

She moaned as she pressed herself against him and he let her take the lead, a novelty for him but he was in such shock that she was so invested in this, that she wanted him this much, that all he could do was run his hands up her back and revel in the feel of her.

On and on she kissed him and he touched her—her back, her hips, her shoulders. Although the chair was awkward for a make-out session, she seemed to fit in his lap, her lips parting and allowing his tongue to roam inside.

They tasted what they could reach of each other, him nuzzling her neck, her earlobe, breathing in the scent of her into his lungs as he traced his fingers over her rib cage. His hands cupped her breasts and his blood sang at her sweet sigh of satisfaction.

His phone rang and he ignored it. This wasn't exactly private, and between her boot and the things he wanted to do to her, he needed more space.

"Hey," he murmured in her ear. "I'm all for this, but we should move to my bedroom. I want to take my time with you, undress you slowly, kiss every inch of you. Run my fingers, as well as my tongue, over every part of you."

She shivered and nipped at his bottom lip. "Keep talking dirty to me and I'll come right here."

Well then.

He found it hard to speak, much less think straight. "Five minutes. Let's go through the photos one more time. Then we'll spend the night together."

"You're kidding, right?" She gave his hard cock, which

was tenting his pants, an exaggerated look. "You're as ready as I am. You can't seriously want to make me wait another five minutes. Do you like torturing people?"

He chuckled. "I've been known to string things out to get what I want, but I would never do that to you."

She blinked and he saw her puzzling out whether this was a confession or a tease. "Good to know."

"I only want you to take a quick look at the photos, not at your dad this time. Please? You've got momentum going with your recall. I want to take advantage of that.

"And then you promise you'll take advantage of me?"

He gently shifted her off his lap and set her into the other chair. It was the hardest thing he'd ever done, but he knew they were onto something and he needed to keep her focused in case this was about to break. "Oh, most definitely."

Reluctantly, she put an elbow on the desk and propped her chin in her hand. "*Three* minutes. That's all you get."

Surreptitiously, he adjusted his pants, trying to release the tight material around his cock. "You're a taskmaster."

She gave a seductive laugh. "Wait until I get you alone."

Watching as he went through each picture, enlarging faces, she used her other hand to rub his thigh. Teasing him. He'd make sure she paid for that once he had her under him.

He was about to say *fuck it,* and whisk her off to his room when she stopped his scrolling. "Wait. Go back."

He did, returning to the previous image. "What is it?"

She pointed. "There. Can you zoom in on that guy?"

He did. The digital photo wasn't the highest quality and became slightly pixelated because the man was in shadows. He tapped a couple keys. "Let me clear it up."

The screen grew fuzzy, then snapped into sharper focus.

"No way." She sat up and a look of horror crossed her face. "That's him."

"Who? Your attacker?"

She shook her head, her terrified eyes meeting his. "That's the man with the scar."

SEVENTEEN

The man in the photo had no visible facial disfigurements. "Are you sure?" Rory asked.

Amelia felt the familiar tug inside her. *Am I?* She'd forgotten so much. Her brain kept playing tricks on her. "I think so." She stopped and gripped the edge of the desk. "No, I'm sure. That's him."

At his extended pause, she poked his arm. "You believe me, don't you?"

"Of course I do. I'm just thinking."

The past seemed to close in on her, her chest growing tight, her throat, thick with emotion, and if she were honest, fear.

"Look, I need to dig into all of this," he said. "Start running facial rec on these people, find out the identities of everyone who was at that party, put everything into our software program. See what comes up."

Oh no. He wasn't getting out of their deal. All of that would take time, possibly days, and he would bury himself in it, just like he always did. She'd seen how he worked a problem, and while she admired his dedication and commitment, she wasn't about to be put on the back burner while he disappeared into a hole. This was her puzzle to figure out. She might not possess the skills he had to uncover the truth, but she planned to be right beside him every step of the way.

At this moment, however, she needed a break. He did, too.

And she knew exactly what would help both of them.

She drew out her cell and texted Beatrice. "The most important thing is to identify that man," she said to Rory. "You have ten minutes to put his face into the recognition software. There are other people in this building who can and will help with the rest. I know you have a hero complex, and you want to figure it out yourself, but, right now, we're going to focus on something else."

"We are?"

She nodded, planted a kiss on him, and headed toward the exit. "Ten minutes, Tephra. As soon as I'm done with you, we'll get back to this."

Inside his room, she took a deep breath, her mind going a million miles an hour. Her dad had been at that event with Hannah's, along with the man with the scar. It was all tied together, and although she didn't know how, she felt better than she had in days. They finally had a lead, and if she could free up her memories, she would figure out what had happened to her in the alley and why. She would also discover what had happened to her father the night of the fire.

Unlocking her brain required unlocking her heart.

She needed to feel confident again, whole again. For a few precious moments, she needed to stop thinking about what had happened—then and now—and distract herself.

In the tiny bathroom she scrubbed her face and took off her clothes. Then she climbed into Rory's bed and waited.

RORY STOPPED OUTSIDE HIS QUARTERS, his mind, as well as his heart, racing. The desire to untwist this puzzle and put the pieces into order gnawed at him.

His desire to please Amelia, to make her his, was forceful.

To ignore her request—no, *demand*—would be agony, and if he was honest with himself, he wasn't strong enough to push it aside.

He needed her. Needed to feel like he wasn't alone anymore.

Yes, he had his brothers. He had Beatrice and Cal. He had the most amazing support team any guy could, but Amelia was...everything.

She'd given him the key to his freedom, getting him back on his feet. The irony was, he didn't want to go anywhere except where she was.

At that moment, she was on the other side of the door.

Don't screw this up. She loves you.

The idea still startled him, even after his discussion with Vivi. Maybe he was lying to himself, because he was the most unlovable of any of them, and through the years, that's the way he'd wanted it to be. He had to bury so much—so much anger. So much frustration. So much dislike for himself.

You're not alone anymore, that voice inside his head said. He couldn't deny it. In his room was the most amazing woman he'd ever met, *and she wants to be with me.*

He attempted to drown out his doubts, his worries. Old habits die hard, but they fled as he forced himself to grab the door knob. *I will not be eighty and regret that I didn't have at least one night with her.*

The room was dark, only a single shaft of light coming in from the window over the bed. Amelia rose like a beautiful shadow, propping herself on an elbow. The sheet fell and her breasts were exposed, creamy and perfect in the light. "You're late," she teased.

Automatically, he checked his watch as he closed the door behind him and locked it. "By one minute."

"With all of this waiting for you,"—she waved a hand over her body. The material draped over her luscious hip and he licked his lips. "I thought you'd be early, eager to get to it."

She had no idea. He yanked off his shirt—might as well get it over with—and she caught her breath at the sight of his scars. "I'm no stunner like the other guys," he admitted, turning, so she could see his back as well. "I've earned each and every one of these babies, and if that makes me a beast to your beauty, then so be it."

"I always loved that story. It was a favorite of mine growing up."

He tried to breathe. "You still want to go through with this?"

"Of course I do, you big dummy."

Steadying his nerves, he shucked off his pants. He braced himself for another gasp at the scars down his legs, but she was quiet.

"Like I said, I've earned every one of them. They each tell a story that I can never escape from. I see them every day and remember how I got them. Vivi claims I should be proud of them, but mostly I use them as reminders of who I used to be and all the things I did. That I can't do anymore.

"Someday I want you to tell me those stories." She patted the bed. "You still have too many clothes on."

The removal of his socks and underwear was quick, and he was already so, so hard. He fumbled with the box of condoms in his nightstand—he'd stolen them from Moe and the kid hadn't even realized it. Yet. It wasn't like Rory was going to run over to the local convenience store and grab some, but the script he'd made as homework from Vivi had included birth control.

Jesus, he felt like a schoolboy with his first girl. But he wanted her to see it all—his secrets, his lust for her—so he stood naked and afraid—okay, maybe he was a bit terrified —in front of her. "I want you to be sure you're here for the right reasons, Amelia. That you want this—me—with your whole heart and body."

Her eyes, dark pools in the shadows, fell to his erection, and she grinned wickedly. "Trust me, I absolutely want this. I want you."

She reached for him then, her warm fingers wrapping around him and he was the one to gasp this time. She tugged him closer, and he leaned down, meeting the lips she turned up to him.

The kiss was sweet and raw and full of hunger. It left him breathless, and her hand, still gripping his cock, began to move.

It all felt so right. *She* felt right. She hadn't been horrified by his body, she wanted to be in his bed.

He tried to think straight, found it impossible. His fingers traveled through her hair and down her neck. He moved onto the mattress on his knees. Her hand increased its rhythm and he wasn't going to need the condom if she kept that up.

Encircling her wrist with his hand, he removed her grip from his cock, then skimmed her ribs, cupped her breast. At his touch, she sighed into his mouth, as if giving him complete and utter control to do whatever he wanted.

He hated himself for stopping that exquisite rhythm of hers, but needed to slow things down. He shifted her so she was under him, and with skilled hands, she removed the condom from the pack and rolled it onto his cock, his groan catching low in his throat.

His mouth claimed hers again, and the smoldering between them erupted into flames. Careful of her injuries, he made sure she was comfortable as she spread her legs and he made his way to her breasts. She smelled like the sea, wild and free, with that layer of lilacs, and he wanted to touch and kiss every inch of her.

Her urgent hands gripped his shoulders, and she drew him up so their mouths met again, fierce, urgent. "Please," she whispered against his lips. "I need you, now."

He stole his fingers down to the apex between her

thighs, his thumb finding the sensitive spot there and causing her to arch. She was indeed wet and ready, and he slipped two inside her. She moaned, deeper this time, and arched even more as he trailed his lips over her neck, whispering all the things he wanted to do to her.

Her nails dug into his back and she widened her legs. "Stop teasing," she ordered. "Get yourself inside me."

Fuck. Just hearing her say it made him nearly climax. He removed his hand from her and palmed himself, guiding the tip of his cock to its destination.

Her hips jerked, sliding up to take him in all the way. His breath hissed out of him and she met his gaze, hers unadulterated, shining with power that she could affect him so.

Turnabout was fair play. Pinning her hands, he smiled into those eyes he loved. "I haven't been with anyone in a long time," he admitted, "but I'll do my best to make you scream my name. To make you happy and satisfy you."

He'd meant it to be a promise, but she saw through the worry still ghosting his words. "You already have," she said.

It was too much. All of it. He kissed her hard, rode her the same, and loved that she gave it all right back to him.

Luckily, he wasn't the only one who was near the limit of what his body could take. Moving with him, stroke for stroke, she caught his bottom lip with her teeth, released it, then murmured, "I can't...hold off...any longer."

Good. That's all he needed to hear. "Come for me, Amelia," he commanded, staring at her. He wanted to see her face when she came, see into her soul.

"Only...if...you...oh, *god*." Panting hard, her muscles

tightened around him like the most delicious of vises. "Come...with...me, Rory!"

Her orgasm struck, her body arching off his bed as he drove himself into her, his own release pumping out of him. Together, they fell off the cliff of joy and pain, love and lust, all mixed together in their hearts and bodies.

EIGHTEEN

T*wo hours later*

"HERE'S WHAT WE KNOW." Beatrice paced from the far end of the conference room to the screen. She pointed to the picture on it. "This man is the alleged leader of an international child abduction ring that has operated since 9/11 across Europe and into North Africa. He started small, but in the past two decades, his targets became those from the top wealthy families in the world."

"Which guarantees him and his crew some very healthy payouts," Moe added. "They only strike every few years, we assume when their funds run low."

Beatrice nodded and went to the next screen. "Interpol arrested these two about seven years ago in an unrelated bust. The FBI believes they have since been replaced by new members, and no matter what they've offered them, they will not give up their cohorts."

Rory and Amelia sat close to each other, their hands and shoulders touching. Rory studied the screen. "Kidnapping? That's what this is about?"

Amelia fidgeted in the chair, causing it to squeak. She switched her attention between him and Beatrice. "I don't understand. What does this have to do with my dad? With the photos on that USB?"

"We're getting to that." Beatrice clicked the remote and the screen switched to the next set of photos. "These are the children they managed to abduct and hold for ransom over the past two decades. The group, nicknamed the Concordia Kidnappers, is highly effective at what they do as well as avoiding capture. We believe the ringleader is Antoni Novak."

"Novak?" Rory frowned. "The jewelry thief?"

"You're thinking of Antolli," Moe said. "That's his brother."

Novak in Poland was like Smith in the USA. "Pre 9/11, Antoni was involved in small time kidnapping and thievery. When the US went to war with Iraq, he saw a golden opportunity to exploit families fleeing the area in search of a new home."

"He'd learned a lot about lifting valuable jewelry from his brother, however," Moe continued. "And when you think about it, both are similar targets: Highly prized but rarely have more than average security around them."

Amelia made a disgusted grunt. "Children are far more valuable than jewelry."

Beatrice didn't miss how Rory squeezed her hand. "To parents like yours, yes. To others?" She shrugged. "Children are easy to locate and track these days, thanks to social media and the fact all of them have cells and other devices. Like Moe said, they have minimal security most of the time." She rested her hands on the back of a chair. "Initially, Antoni concentrated in the Middle East and North Africa but still returned to Poland on occasion. One of those jobs involved Rena Zelinska. She was fifteen and on the run from her family, who owned several factories in Poland. He believed they were rich, but he failed to do enough due diligence to discover they were on the brink of bankruptcy. Her parents couldn't pay the ransom he requested, and instead of killing her, he kept her."

"*Kept* her?" Amelia looked horrified. "Like a prisoner? A sex slave?"

"The authorities believe it was consensual." Beatrice gave her what she hoped was a reassuring smile. "I know this is hard to hear, but it does happen."

Amelia dropped her gaze. "Sorry. It's just..."

"Don't apologize." Beatrice found it tough to not get emotional about these types of things, too, especially now that she was a mother. They both had to stay detached, though, in order to not end up in a quagmire of useless, even if it was heartfelt, sadness. Amelia had walked into this meeting with a bit of bounce in her step, and it was good to see, but if she got too emotional over the information Beatrice and Moe were about to present, it wouldn't help any of them. "Please remember that we can't change the past, only affect the future. And that's why we're here.

It's quite possible this ring is planning another abduction, and soon."

Amelia paled. "Are you serious?"

"You may have uncovered something of national importance," Moe told her.

Beatrice nodded at Amelia's questioning glance. "Antoni trained Rena and they ran a bunch of cons, stealing jewelry and art, as well as kidnapping kids. They brought on a co-conspirator whose name and identity have never been verified. An unknown but powerful person whom the authorities suspect moves in higher-end circles and has access to rich and famous families."

"How do they know this person joined them if they don't know who he is?" Amelia asked.

"The MO changed," Moe said. "Originally, Antoni and Rena were targeting easy kids, but low risk, low reward. When the third twit came onboard, they began going after bigger gains."

"Which meant higher risk, so they added yet another partner. One highly trained in security measures and able to avoid even the best of those." Beatrice hit the remote. A new set of faces peered back at them. "These are potential candidates, because again, we don't have confirmation. The group wears disguises, uses false identities, and they stay off the radar."

Amelia's spine went ramrod straight. "Wait. *That's* one of them?"

"Potentially," Moe said, eyeing the man with the scar. "After the Concordia hijacking, the heat was on. They didn't get all the ransoms they asked for, but they earned enough that the group broke up for a period of years.

Interpol and the Feds suspect at least two bopped over here to America."

Rory made a note on his laptop. "Concordia, I remember that. A bus of kids from a British military boarding school was hijacked and six of them kidnapped. That's when this group was dubbed with that name by the press."

"They ranged in age from ten to fourteen." Moe stared at the table in front of him. "The bastards held them at gunpoint, brutally beat them, tied them up." His voice went low, all trace of accent disappearing. "One boy died trying to save the others."

Beatrice shot Rory a look, hoping to telegraph the importance of that last sentence.

Rory caught her stare, his attention zeroing in on Moe. "You knew him?"

Moe's Adam's apple bobbed. His chin jerked. "Not important."

"The fuck it isn't." Rory snapped a finger at him, earning him a glare when Moe met his eyes. "Did you attend the Academy?"

"You're a tosser, you know that?"

"I'm worse than that." Rory dropped the antagonism and leaned on the table. "You were close?"

"He was my brother."

Amelia gasped and reached for Moe's arm. "Moe, I'm so sorry."

Rory blew out an audible breath. "Shit, you fucker. Why didn't you tell me? Jesus." He rubbed a hand over his face. "It's not in your dossier. That sucks beyond words."

Moe's jaw flexed, eyes darting to the corner of the

room as he made a dismissive gesture. "Like B said, we can't change the past."

The unsaid and unresolved grief in the room pressed on Beatrice. Solving this case and nailing someone—*anyone* —involved in that ring could bring him some closure. She flipped to the next screen. "The FBI had an interest in our Bluebird mystery man, who went by Jan Meidros and lived in a small town south of the North Carolina border."

"Near us?" Amelia asked.

Beatrice nodded. "Back then, a local sheriff stopped him for a broken taillight, nothing alarming, but when they found a bag with clothes, cash, and several unregistered guns in a hidden compartment in the trunk, they arrested him. He was flagged by the Feds, but they had bigger things on their plate at that time. In court, the case was thrown out due to an overzealous deputy violating Jan's rights during the arrest. He was once again in the wind."

Moe raised a sheet of paper. "Until...a few weeks later when his fake ID was used to rent a car at the airport. Some grunt in an FBI cubicle put him on their watch list. It was happening to hundreds of innocent people at that time, but a few wankers were tagged as well."

"After reading up on all of this, here's what I think." Beatrice brought up a photo of the sanctuary event showing their suspect and Amelia's father, Baron Thorpe. "I reached out to one of my contacts at The Bureau. Your dad was a CI for the local branch in Columbia. Like all law enforcement, they were recruiting at that time, hoping to prevent further terrorist attacks on US soil. And they did. Your father, however, was put on Jan's trail."

"Wait." Amelia blinked. "My dad was an informant for the FBI?"

"Plenty of patriotic folks volunteered then and some were recruited."

She shook her head in disbelief. "That can't be. My mom would've known, wouldn't she?"

"Unlikely," Rory said. "They would have insisted he keep it a secret."

"He was a WL—instructed to Watch and Listen only," Beatrice told her. "Jan lived half a mile from you and your dad passed his house daily. According to the file, Baron alerted them to Jan's comings and goings when he observed them. He made notes about anyone he saw Jan meet with."

"This is *not* possible." Amelia gripped the table, her voice barely above a whisper as realization sunk in. "My dad was a spy."

"And a good one according to my contact. He had a notebook full of Jan's movements and had added pages of his own theories about what the man was up to."

Rory put an arm around her shoulders before he asked Beatrice, "What happened the night of the event?"

"I think Jan saw an easy score—plenty of the local wealthy citizens supporting the fundraiser, and then, like a gift from the heavens, the then-governor Clemson dropped into his lap, along with his daughter."

"Hannah?" Amelia recoiled. "He was going to kidnap her?"

"Yes." Beatrice placed the remote on the table and pulled out her chair. "I think your father stopped him."

Moe waggled a finger at his own face. "I fancy a wager that's where he got the scar."

"Why would my dad let him into our house, then? Why didn't he call the police?"

"We may never know for sure," Beatrice admitted. "The agent who recruited him was transferred shortly after the fundraiser and died a few months later from a brain aneurysm. Most likely, he'd told your father not to engage Jan, and if your dad *did* give the man that scar, the agent may have decided to cut ties. Too risky to have an untrained, unofficial CI engaging criminals and getting into altercations."

"Were there any incident reports about fights or attempted kidnappings that evening?" Rory asked.

Moe shook his head. "Although the copper who let Jan slip through his fingers due to his overzealous arrest *was* on duty that night and worked the party alongside the governor's police detail. We can't rule out that he may have also taken Jan to task, or at least kept any fisticuffs between Jan and Amelia's pop a secret."

"What about Masden and the other agents?" Rory asked. "Anything on them?"

Amelia sat back, eyes widening. "You ran background checks on Hannah's Secret Service agents?"

Beatrice slid a paper down the table to them. "As you can see, they came up squeaky clean, as expected. Rory stated there was some concern about Agent Masden, but we found nothing to raise suspicions about him."

"Doesn't mean he didn't snatch the purse," Rory said, reading the paper over Amelia's shoulder. "Why do you think anyone would want to steal those pictures?"

"To keep a secret hidden." Beatrice toyed with her pen. "We just have to figure out what that secret is. My guess? The unidentified co-conspirator is in at least one of those pictures. He or she is still active in this ring, and they don't want to be found out."

"You think that's who attacked me?" Amelia's shock was growing. "I'm scared to even think about this, but..." She swallowed and set her face. "Why didn't this guy kill me if he thought I could out him?"

"Because you can't do it without the pictures," Rory told her. "One of the most important tricks of the trade, whether you're a criminal or a spy, is not to use overkill for a problem. Literally. Homicide brings too much heat. Make it look like a mugging and the police won't give it more than fifteen minutes of their attention before the next crime draws them away."

"My concern right now is a big one." Beatrice tapped her pen. "It's quite possible they're planning something for Thursday night."

"At the fundraiser?" Amelia looked sick. "You mean kidnapping. All those kids. But...most of them aren't from wealthy families."

Rory swore under his breath. "Their sponsors are. It's the perfect setup to grab at least one of their kids, if not more."

"Especially if the whole gang is in on it," Moe added.

Beatrice's skin crawled. "I'm working on tightening security by placing some of our Rock Stars in amongst the other bodyguards, but it has to stay under the radar. We don't want to alert our insider. He or she has to be someone who has the confidence and trust of Hannah, and possibly her parents."

"Doesn't matter who it is, or if the Concordias are all here." Moe stood, his face a thundercloud. "We're going to be there to stop them."

NINETEEN

T *hursday night*

THE TORINA PAVILION and Commerce Center was packed by the time Amelia and Rory arrived. Cars came and went, dropping off passengers who streamed across the expansive lawn and sidewalk lighted by modern solar lights and accented with natural plants.

Ahead of them, Connor stopped under the awning at the rear of the building for Cal and Beatrice to get out, the two of them seemingly at ease. There was too much hoopla out front with media outlets and paparazzi, and most in SFI preferred to keep a low profile. Rory would gladly stay under his rock and observe from the comfort of the Bat Cave, if not for Amelia.

Cal, filling his tux like it was a second skin, held out a hand to assist Beatrice from the seat. The golden chiffon of her gown flowed over her and her side swept updo was held in place by a comb that acted as a lock pick and weapon should she need it. It had been designed by Rory himself.

Tate Warren, acting as Rory and Amelia's chauffeur, spoke into his comm unit. "Testing One-Two-Three. You guys good? Over."

Rory's nerves jangled. "Yes, for the fifth time, we're fucking good. We hear you loud and clear."

Amelia giggled and he wiped the glare he was sending the rookie from the backseat off his face before he peeked at her. Gorgeous in a deep plum colored dress that fell to her ankles and covered most of the boot, she'd left her hair down and the natural curls brushed her bare shoulders. She'd chosen a sparkling choker and matching bracelet from Beatrice's collection, both items containing a combo GPS tracker, microphone, and camera.

She quirked a brow at Rory, humorous chastisement dancing in her eyes. He wanted to simply stare at her, skip this event, and whisk her back to the safety of SFI, but he knew how important tonight was. Not just to her, but all of them.

Him included, as Vivi had brazenly pointed out earlier that day when she'd come to see him. "This will be a good test for you," she'd said. "Think of it as a celebration of how far you've come."

"I have a mission," he'd growled. "It's not a party for me. We have to catch this guy and break up the kidnapping ring."

She held up a finger. "*If* he's there and you can figure out who he is. You'll have every one of us backing you up, so the whole thing isn't on you. Lighten up a bit. Let yourself enjoy the night and your date."

"It's not a date." He'd convinced himself that since they might possibly catch a kidnapper, and potentially Amelia's attacker, it was a *job*. A mission. "I'm her bodyguard. That's how I have to look at it."

Vivi had offered a tolerant smile. "We still have a lot of work to do on you, don't we?"

His short temper had risen quickly, but she'd turned and waved over her shoulder before disappearing.

Reluctantly, he switched his gaze to Tate. "Sorry, man. I'm keyed up. I don't do well with crowds." A worn out excuse, yet still true.

"No prob, Bob," the kid said, and Rory wanted to kill him all over again. "Perimeter is secure and we have all of you inside looking out for those kids. Connor and I are on surveillance with Trace for the exits after we park. We aren't using the garage next door, btw. Too crowded and access is challenging due to the elevators, so the vehicles will be two blocks over in a municipal lot. We won't let anything happen; I swear on my tadpole tattoo."

Which was no doubt on his ass, a typical spot for them.

And wasn't *that* an image Rory didn't want in his head.

"Do you all get them?" Amelia asked as they came to a stop under the awning. Pillars wrapped with tiny white lights held it up. Others twinkled on the living tree sculptures lining the sidewalk. It was more than Rory expected but nothing like the overdone decor out front. "The frog tattoos?"

"Used to be they frowned upon them," Tate said. "It made us too identifiable to the enemy. These days, you'd be hard-pressed to find one of us that doesn't have at least one, if not a dozen."

Things had definitely changed since Rory's stint in the SEALs. He popped the door. "Don't worry about me. You keep your eyes on Amelia at all times, you hear me, tadpole?"

Tate gave him a mock salute. "Roger that to the tenth, sir."

Because of the smartass tone, Rory made a mental note to knock him in the head later. He took a deep breath and put on his game face before he exited the vehicle, casually scanning the area as he buttoned his jacket. He took in every detail before he offered Amelia his hand.

As she accepted, wrangling her single crutch out of the back along with her purse, he monitored his watch, showing him video of Moe and Parker waiting in the line of cars out front. Through his open window, Moe handed a member of the parking staff his keys and the man held up a cell, sending the coordinating code for pickup to the phone Moe extended. No paper tickets or other physical markers—it was all done these days by text and bots. Technology was a wonderful thing.

Amelia juggled her purse—the exact replica of the stolen one. Rory had put a tracking device inside the lining of it, and he helped her as she fiddled with the hook and strap Sabrina had designed for it to attach to her crutch.

He angled his body like a shield, keeping his beautiful date between him and the car and assisting as best he could.

There was no one back here except Cal and Beatrice, along with a single attendant Hannah had posted for them, but his two bosses inconspicuously did the same, shielding Amelia and keeping their backs to the security camera. It wasn't that any of them felt an immediate threat, it was simply second nature to close ranks around one of their own.

"Got you on my radar," a familiar voice said in Rory's ear. Trace was on a nearby rooftop with a sniper rifle and scope. "All clear. No suspicious activity to report."

"Roger that," Cal replied under his breath.

Rory had a fold-up cane inside his jacket, which was cumbersome, but he didn't want to get caught without it. Plus, a prop like that could come in handy if tonight went sideways. The cane had some of that amazing technology embedded in it, and when extended and locked, became a useful weapon. Bonus—he'd glued Batman to the top. A true nerd move, but he didn't give a damn.

He kept a hand on Amelia's lower back to steady her as they moved toward the waiting staff member who would check them in. The decked out crutch had been painted gold and sported enough pink rhinestones to gag a horse.

While Amelia had argued to leave it behind, they had all insisted she display it and use it to her advantage. The purse as well. If her attacker was here, she needed to appear vulnerable, and like Rory's cane, the crutch might come in handy to fend him off.

Her bag contained a taser as well, along with a normal collection of things women tended to carry.

He also kept a hand on her because he needed to. *Wanted* to. She had quickly become the most important thing in his life and he never wanted to be far from her. His goal was to touch her every chance he got.

They heard the thump of music; an upbeat dance tune being played by a DJ who was part of Hannah's Leading Edge program. The wide glass door was opened by the attendant, who smiled and greeted them, marking a list on her computer tablet when Rory showed her their digital tickets.

"Ms. Clemson will be delighted you made it," the attendant said. "Turn left at the Three Muses statue and you'll see the reception area. Champagne and canapés are being served—I highly recommend the smoked salmon pastries—and the event officially kicks off in ten minutes. Enjoy!"

"I'll escort you." Secret Security Agent Masden appeared, looking them over. "Ms. Clemson has asked me to."

Rory went on alert. At the same time, he felt Amelia stiffen. "That's not necessary," she told him with a lift of her chin.

He glanced at the blinged-out crutch and her foot, which peeked from the hem of her dress. "I'm also instructed to apologize for my rude behavior." The words seemed pulled from him with pliers but he kept his face expression-free. "I'm...*enthusiastic,* as she terms it, about keeping her safe. I...she's..."

The detached look melted into something akin to stifled embarrassment. The tenseness left Amelia's body. "I suppose that's a good thing," she said. "You care for her, don't you?"

He glanced down. "That obvious?"

She grinned. "Does she know?"

Rory glanced at Cal and Beatrice. Cal shrugged, perplexed. Beatrice smiled.

"No, and please don't tell her," Masden said, face now awash in concern. "If she finds out, I'll be transferred." He removed a towel from his pocket. "One clean dishtowel returned."

Amelia laughed and accepted it, tucking it into her bag. "You're forgiven and your secret is safe with us."

The man gave a half bow and disappeared.

"What just happened?" Rory asked.

"He's in love with her." Amelia's smile was full of whimsy and longing. "Isn't it romantic?"

He and Cal again shared a look of *what the fuck* and Rory shook it off. "She doesn't share his feelings, though." He almost felt sorry for the guy. He had to admit, he understood his gruff manner a bit better now. He was the same around Amelia. "I don't think that's romantic."

"But I think she does," Amelia argued. As they crossed the threshold, the music grew louder. "She told me she'd fallen for someone but couldn't talk about him. Her father would freak out. I thought it was a man on the other side of the political fence, but maybe it's Masden."

Beatrice slipped an arm through Cal's. "That is romantic. Wait until I tell Vivi. She loves stories like this."

Rory let it go as the two couples made their way to the designated meeting point far from the cameras and reporters vying for an interview with D.C.'s up-and-coming, as well as the already rich and famous. The itch between his shoulders came to life.

TWENTY

"You look like someone killed your dog," Amelia said. "Stop grinding your teeth."

He forced a chuckle, covertly taking in the security cameras tucked in the ceiling corners and scanning the dozens of faces filing past. He took her free arm and tucked it inside his. "Have I told you how beautiful you look tonight?"

"About five times." She winked with an evil grin. "But unlike you with Tate, I love that you're making sure I've heard you."

His chuckle turned real. "I probably deserved that."

Beatrice watched them with a knowing smile. "Inside joke?"

Amelia grinned. "One of many." She used her chin to denote the stream of folks heading into the main room. "What do you think?"

Parker and Moe joined them, him visually sweeping the area as Rory had done.

"I think our male companions need to stop being so conspicuous." Beatrice cocked her updo to the left. "There's Sabrina. Everyone act casual. Like this is fun and not as if you're having a root canal."

Her voice was in his ear as well as next to him, the order going out to all of them over their comms. Sabrina, in a caterer's black and white outfit, sauntered up with a tray of champagne flutes. Her hair was in a slicked back bun and she wore no eye makeup. "Good evening. May I interest any of you in a drink?"

Beatrice and Amelia took a glass. Cal and Rory did not. Moe took two. "What?" he asked to the brows that went up, downing the content of one in a long gulp. "You said act like we're having fun."

Sabrina grinned. Parker elbowed him. "Top of your game, Henley," she growled, using his Rock Star nickname. "Not drunk off your ass."

"Don't worry," Sabrina said with gusto. "It's sparkling white grape juice. For the underage crowd. Not a drop of liquor in it."

Moe pursed his lips and made smacking sounds as he returned the empty to the tray. "I knew that. It's not bloody likely I'd get trollied on the job now, is it? Blimey, Parker. Have a tad bit of faith." He glanced at Cal. "Shall we crack on, then?"

Cal, ever stoic, pasted on a fake smile that Rory knew well—he hated this charade as much as Rory did. "I count six cameras and three security guards. Coldplay? You read us?"

"Roger that," Trace replied. "All systems go. We have eyeballs on you."

Rory's patch into the main security system had been deemed necessary and he was relieved it was giving those not inside the hall with them the layout. Not that he'd thought it wouldn't, but he'd had to work around another interested party who'd piggybacked onto it as well. Might be the Secret Service, might be the kidnappers. Either way, he'd had to ghost his feed so it didn't alert any of them.

"In we go," Beatrice said. "Vivi and Ian are already here. Each of you has your assignment."

Amelia tensed under his possessive hand, then blew out a breath and returned her untouched flute to Sabrina's tray. She and Rory were on Hannah duty; Cal and B would be watching the donors, specifically any who interacted with the Leading Edge entrepreneurs. Parker and Moe were to observe the influencers. Vivi and Ian were to keep their focus on the various security details. Sabrina was there to eavesdrop on gossip and be general backup.

All were watching the kids, both those in LEAD and those of the wealthy gathered to support them. Children were taught to trust law enforcement, firefighters, and others in uniform, and in the event they became separated from their parents, they could easily be lead away by a kidnapper posing as one.

"Running facial rec on our Keystone Cops," Connor told them. He, Tate, and the rest of Trace's team were set up in a three-layered perimeter. They covered all exits, parking lots, and escape routes.

While Rory felt like his bowtie—the real deal he'd had to break down and ask Amelia to help him do—was choking him, the rush of being on a mission had his pulse beating faster with anticipation. It had been a long fucking time since he'd had this level of involvement in an undercover sting operation. He was torn between being happy about an altercation and scared witless. He had to keep Amelia safe and he'd made her recite his four main tenants until he'd driven her to the point of impatience and she'd flipped him off.

He slid a finger to his comm and turned it off before leaning close and murmuring in her ear, "You remember what I taught you?"

"How could I forget?" When she saw his pointed look, she rolled her eyes, limping along beside him. Her voice became mechanical. "Don't go anywhere alone. Know where the closest exit is at all times. Report anything suspicious. If something goes down, do not engage and get to safety."

Inside the main hall, at least a hundred folks meandered about, visiting with the Leading Edge members who had booths set up along two walls, and searching for their assigned seats at tables covered with fancy cloths.

Each booth and every table showcased one of the night's kids, complete with information cards listing their bio and accomplishments to date.

The four of them found their assigned seats as a woman took the stage and calmed the crowd. She welcomed them and offered a preview of the evening's itinerary, making sure to compliment the event coordinators and throwing in a plug for donations before she introduced Hannah.

The First Daughter looked at home as she strode

across the stage, acknowledged the applause, then focused everyone's attention on the reason they were there.

A natural at speeches, she peppered hers with antidotes and puns, explaining the reason she'd started Leading Edge, the successes they'd had in the few short years since its inception, and how important bringing brilliant young minds together on a world stage was. "After all," Hannah said, smiling out at the gathering, "child inventors have been improving our lives for years, bringing us things like earmuffs, the trampoline, and even Christmas lights. Let's support these youth tonight and encourage our leaders of tomorrow!"

Applause swept the room, accompanied by cheers and whistles. Hannah introduced the first of three presenters, a thirteen-year-old who had invented a bicycle for paraplegics. Her younger brother had incurred a spinal injury and since his favorite thing was to ride his bike, she'd tinkered with various versions until she'd found one that worked with a combination of hand pedaling and verbal commands.

The next was a sophomore in college who'd developed a skin patch for burn victims that kept their wounds bacteria free and improved healing time by weeks, all based on shark skin properties. She was working on various skin tone adjustments so the patches would blend into the user's own coloring.

By the third and final presenter—a fifteen-year-old social media star who had developed a language learning system that made use of colors and shapes, along with musical notes, to help people with reading and speaking multiple languages, Rory found it challenging not to be engrossed by each of their ideas. The current one was teaching the crowd basic French—masculine and feminine nouns, verb conjugation and more, using a color matching system. She already had several companies interested in patenting it for use with the under-five crowd, as a second language aid, and for those with certain reading disabilities.

It literally *could* change the world.

He bobbed his knee under the table, clapping along with the others as the final presenter finished. His attention naturally jumped to the booths as folks rose from their seats to meet the kids and learn about their talents. So far, nothing and no one had appeared out of place.

So far.

Moe attacked another plate of appetizers. "This is proper good nosh, innit?"

"Can you speak English for once?" Rory growled.

"I speak it all the time, you bloody pillock. If you recall, the British had the market on the language long before you ungrateful upstarts came along."

"*I'm* an idiot?" Moe seemed surprised he knew the meaning of pillock and Rory gave him a knowing smile. "Take a look in the mirror, you ugly prat."

"Ha!" Moe laughed, wiping his fingers on a posh napkin as he leaned back in his chair. "Mildly offensive, mate."

He'd give him offensive. As soon as they got out of here.

"Enough," Parker warned. "Both of you."

Beatrice made a slashing motion with her finger across

her throat as Hannah and a dark haired man arrived at their table.

"Amelia," Hannah cooed, bending down to kiss her cheek. "I'm so happy you made it! How are you feeling?"

"Good." Amelia's smile was genuine. "Tonight is wonderful. You did a great job organizing this."

"I had a lot of help." She wasn't wearing the brace but had a flesh-colored wrap on her wrist. She eyed Rory. "You clean up nice."

He bit his tongue, forced a smile.

She returned her attention to Amelia. "Did you see Binni? She's here somewhere."

The purse sat on the table in plain view, Amelia's crutch under her chair. "Not yet. The presentations were fabulous. I want to learn French now in the worst way."

Hannah laughed, pointing at the purse. "Is that the one that was stolen? Did they capture your mugger?"

"Not yet," Amelia said. "This is my extra. I checked it and found that USB."

"You did? Did you look at the pictures?"

She nodded. "That's definitely my dad. Thank you for sharing them. It was so good to see his face again."

"Where are my manners?" Hannah turned to her companion. "Chad, this is Amelia, the friend I was telling you about. Amelia, this is Chad LeFarre."

"Holy fuck," Tate said in Rory's ear. "He's a tech billionaire. Lives in France. Rarely leaves his compound. What's *he* doing here?"

Rory closed his eyes for a heartbeat, wishing he could reach through the earbud and silence the kid. For good measure and to relieve his annoyance, he kicked Moe under the table instead.

"Ow! Hey," Moe sputtered, nearly choking on his chipotle wings dipped in some fancy-ass sauce. "What the bloody hell?"

Rory acted innocent and when the others ignored the exchange, Hannah introduced Chad to them.

The Rolex on the guy's wrist was worth more than all the cars they'd arrived in. Rory came to his feet, uncomfortable with Chad looking down on him as they shook hands.

Cal did the same, then walked a few feet away, pretending to peruse a handout from one of the booths. "Run this guy through our main program," he murmured to the team. "Now."

Chad took Amelia's hand, bending over it and giving her a sultry look, a lock of his hair falling across his forehead. "Nice to meet you, Ms. Thorpe."

He knew her last name? Had Hannah mentioned it previously, because she hadn't just now. Rory balled his hands into fists and felt Beatrice tug on his jacket to get him to sit.

It took every ounce of willpower to do so.

"I'm certainly glad you made it after what happened," he said in a voice like warm brandy. Rory noted his accent was subdued. Also, fake as hell. "Hannah told me you were attacked. That you have memory issues. Sounds terrible, but you're obviously not one to let it get you down."

Amelia withdrew her hand. "I'm tougher than I look

and my memory is coming back—not only about that night, but other things as well."

If Rory hadn't been in love with her before, he was now.

She scrutinized Chad's face, hers absent of any fear. "Have we met before? You look familiar."

He didn't miss a beat. "*Mais, non.* I would remember such a lovely *femme.* Perhaps you've seen my photo in a magazine."

"Huh." She continued to stare at him, narrowing her eyes. "Are you investing in one of Hannah's kids?"

"He's selected three," Hannah interjected, nearly bouncing with excitement. "Kenesha's one of them. Isn't that wonderful?"

Chad smiled smugly. "I do what I can for our youth." He winked at Hannah and took her injured hand gently between both of his. "And for those I consider good friends."

Hannah blinked, and Rory mentally groaned. This was the guy she was nuts about, not the Secret Service agent.

Chad excused himself and Hannah watched him go. A line of people had formed behind her, many in the crowd wanting to speak with her and take selfies. A couple instantly took Chad's place, drawing her into a conversation.

"Keep eyes on him," Rory murmured, dropping into his chair once more. "And run that smug face against Amelia's photos."

Amelia dropped her gaze to the table. "I'm sure he's right. We've never met. But there's *something* about him."

There sure was. "Like he's a privileged a-hole?" Rory commented.

"He's only been pictured in a few magazines in recent years," Tate told them. "Mostly regarding his philanthropy and his bachelor status."

Before any of them could comment further, Hannah introduced the couple who'd demanded her attention. They smiled and nodded politely, but the man brought up the president's latest speech on state taxation and began trying to pressure Hannah to sway him to the other side.

"Harold, you know my policy is no politics." She smiled graciously and drew them away as she pointed them to one of the booths. "Tonight isn't about that, and I have no pull with the president, I assure you."

Amelia lifted her crutch from beneath her seat, angling it free from the legs. She spoke to Beatrice and Parker. "Powder room for me. Anyone else?"

Rory shot to his feet, but Beatrice motioned for him to sit. "We've got this."

"I'm her bodyguard. Where she goes, I go."

She laid a hand on his shoulder. "Parker and I can handle it."

Amelia nodded. "We'll be right back. I promise."

His shoulder blades twitched. Out of the corner of his eye, he saw Cal and Moe exchange a look.

Fuck. He was overreacting.

Again.

Beatrice, Vivi, and Amelia were three grown women, two of whom were highly trained and could probably whip his ass on any given day. They were surrounded by SFI employees and security.

But then Beatrice said, "Bring the bag," and Rory's stomach plunged.

"Why?" he demanded, sure he already knew the answer. She wanted to taunt Amelia's attacker if he was here.

And if Masden *wasn't* their man, who was?

Had that stupid show at the door earlier been just that—a show Masden had put on to cover his ass?

Or were they still blind to who else was hunting for those pictures?

"Because." Beatrice said, snapping Rory out of his circling thoughts. "Women take their purses to the restroom. We're going for normal. Remember?"

Moe snorted, and this time, Rory reached over and boxed his ears.

TWENTY-ONE

"I knew he'd be intense," Parker said as they left the main floor, the DJ starting a fresh round of music, "but yeesh."

Amelia nodded, barely leaning on her crutch. "He's really worried about me." Beatrice had warned the rest of the team they would be turning off their comms for this foray, which Amelia was thankful for. No way did she want a dozen men listening in while she peed. She'd do her business as quickly as possible, knowing this would add yet another layer to Rory's anxiety. Problem was, there was a line. "Did you know about Moe and his brother?"

Parker focused on digging a lipstick out of her handbag. "Not until you uncovered all this." She shot a glance to Beatrice. "It does explain a few things."

"I couldn't volunteer that kind of information," Beatrice said quietly. "Not even Rory knew."

"I'm not blaming you. He should have told me himself. Another example of how he doesn't ever let his guard totally down."

Vivi joined them, slipping her earbud into her silver clutch. "Those kids are flippin' incredible, aren't they?"

"Aren't you glad you came?" Amelia asked, letting go of the Moe conversation. It was nice interacting with these women she so admired, and she had faith that Parker would figure things out with Moe.

"Absolutely."

"Moe and Rory aren't that different," Beatrice went on. "On every personality test and evaluation performed on Rory during his years with our military and government, do you know what he scored highest in? Loyalty. And that equates to protection. He'll do anything to safeguard and defend those he cares about. I hired him to watch over me and my family, but also to extend that level of loyalty and protection to those I hired at SFI. He may be over-vigilant and ornery, but he will do everything in his power to keep each and every one of us safe. Same for Moe. They have their shields—Rory uses anger; Moe prefers sarcasm and pretends to be aloof—but underneath those facades are the bravest of warriors. Courageous, indomitable men."

"Amen to that," Vivi said.

Parker stayed silent. Amelia felt proud.

Laughter broke out at the far end of the line. Vivi pointed at Amelia's crutch. "Sabrina did a bang-up job. Everyone's talking about you and that bling-y thing."

"They are?"

"You may have started a new trend," Parker said with a wink. "Next thing we know, you'll be looking for investors."

"I'd much rather be known as the PT who got Rory walking again." She nodded at Vivi. "Along with your help, of course."

"He's definitely nailing his stretch goal tonight," the psychologist said. "He even trimmed his beard."

"He has product in his hair," Beatrice added with a grin. "I can hardly believe it's the same man."

Amelia felt her own smile growing. "Loyal and handsome. A winning combination."

"Not to take the spotlight off him," Vivi muttered, turning serious, "but Ian's acting weird. He keeps denying it, but I think he's got spying in his blood now and he won't quit. He stink eyes every single person who passes us like they're a criminal. It's driving me crazy."

"The sweet taste of success," Parker mused. "Let me tell you, it's a rush. Give him time. He'll settle down."

"He claims one of the men at the table in front of us makes his warning bells go off."

"Half the people here do that to me," Beatrice confided. "He didn't say anything on comms."

"Probably because he knows he sounds paranoid." Vivi huffed. "I asked him if he thought we should alert you all, but he said no. I hope he doesn't decide to play hero and blow our cover over nothing."

Nobody was paying attention as they moved another step forward, the ladies in front of them talking and laughing in Chinese and a tipsy older woman behind them gossiping on her phone to someone named Carl. She kept raising her voice, insisting he needed to get there quick and sponsor a boy who'd created an app to help folks with Alzheimer's recognize their loved ones.

"Rory will kill him if he does," Amelia said.

"And then I'll have to kill Rory." Vivi sighed dramatically. "Such a mess. I hope there's plenty of woods at the new compound for the bodies."

They all laughed and then their conversation turned to the presenters, the food, and the array of designer clothes, shoes, and handbags in the place. Beatrice volunteered that she and Amelia believed Hannah's agent was in love with her.

"Classic," Vivi said. "Someone should make a movie."

"Tonight is a jewelry thief's dream," Parker said. "Did you see that emerald Senator Ralston is wearing?"

They each mentioned their favorite gowns and shoes.

Vivi asked, "I haven't seen Binni, have you, Amelia?"

She shook her head. "Hannah said she's here."

Beatrice stilled. "Have you met her before, this designer?"

"Not in person. Why?"

She frowned, moving with the line as several women emerged from the restroom and they finally neared the door. "Just curious."

It was more than that from the look on her face.

"She's rather reclusive from what I've read," Parker said. "She only makes guest appearances on occasion. Claims she has some kind of people phobia."

"Anthropophobia?" At Parker's nod, Vivi *hmm*ed. "Interesting."

"She's also an artist." Amelia didn't know why she felt

the need to defend the woman. "I'm sure she'd rather be in her studio creating new designs than kibitzing with the likes of us. She's building an empire and that takes a lot of energy."

After they were done, they headed back, Vivi splitting off as they entered the main hall.

Rory came to his feet, wiping his brow with his cloth napkin the moment he spotted her. "Everything okay?" he asked as she neared.

The sheer worry on his face made her feel a tiny bit guilty for putting him through the radio silence, even if it had been fun to chitchat with the others like it was a normal evening of frivolity. "I'm fine," she insisted. "Where's Moe?"

"He left," Cal volunteered. "People tend to do that when they're smacked upside the head."

"He needed it." Rory helped her into her chair and settled the crutch under it. "He better be glad I'm in therapy or I'd do more than that to him."

The plates had been cleared and she set her purse in front of her. People were continuing to socialize but the crowd had thinned slightly. Sabrina swept by, removing empty glasses from the table next to them and offering coffee.

"Any interest in the bag?" Rory asked.

"None." She looked for her friend, but Hannah was nowhere in sight. "Tomorrow, you apologize first thing to Moe. Take him to lunch or something. Tate, too."

Parker, sipping water, choked and set down the glass. "I'd like to be a fly on the wall during that interaction."

Sabrina snorted.

Rory scowled, but at Amelia's glare, relented. "I'll apologize but I'm not taking him to lunch."

She patted his hand, wondering if they needed to keep this up. Stay any longer. Maybe their ruse had been for nothing. "All quiet still?"

"Not a peep," Cal said. He watched a woman wearing a vintage style skirt that looked like it should have a poodle sewn on it. She was talking loudly in an upper East Coast nasally accent and gesturing at Kenesha's digital screen that ran a program highlighting her projects. The woman's son, about eight, sidled away, playing a game on his phone. Kenesha looked like she wished the ground would open up and swallow her. Or maybe the woman.

"Let's run interference," Beatrice suggested, grabbing Cal's arm and tugging him to his feet. "I'd like to see what photos she's used in her video. Parker?"

She lifted one of the full water glasses. "I'm on it."

Amelia stared in wonder as Parker "accidentally" tripped, splashing the liquid on the woman's shoes. Cal and Beatrice moved her off to the side, grabbing napkins and calling for the nearest server, who just happened to be Sabrina, to assist in cleaning things up. Meanwhile, Parker engaged the young boy in a chat, keeping an eye on him.

"This was a bust, wasn't it?" Amelia asked Rory. "All of this manpower and we came up empty-handed."

"You didn't think our suspect would get up on stage and announce himself, did you?"

She fiddled with her necklace. "No, but we haven't even got a hit with all of your sophisticated facial recognition software."

"Night's not over. Takes time for it to do its thing

comparing this many people against the photos in the dozens of databases we have."

She narrowed her eyes. "You're still hoping for a takedown."

"Hell, yeah, I am. I didn't get dressed up in this monkey suit for..." He stopped, seemed to think better of it. Removed his comm and lowered his voice. "I got dressed up for *you*, but I'm open to being rewarded. I mean—"

She covered her comm. "I know what you mean and your reward is coming," she teased. "I promise."

Hannah suddenly appeared, rushing over before he could kiss her. "Binni has to take off and I told her she can't leave until she meets you. She's waiting in the curator's office. Come on. She has that bag she promised."

Amelia clapped her hands. Yes! She was finally going to meet the designer and add a new purse to her collection. "Excellent."

Rory helped her to her feet. Together they followed Hannah from the main room, Cal and Beatrice tailing them from a discreet distance.

They passed Masden manning the entrance to the office. Binni paced at the far end in a black and white men's suit, talking to someone on the phone in Korean. A bold hat with a peacock feather sat on top of a gorgeous red box. She gave a curt wave and smiled at them but kept talking and pacing.

Amelia had a dozen questions for Hannah, least of which was about Chad. Probably better to start with the one she couldn't stop thinking about. She checked to make sure the door was firmly closed. "Did you realize Masden is in love with you?"

Hannah drew back. "What?"

"He is." Amelia felt terrible for the guy—it had been obvious Hannah had a thing for the billionaire. "I thought you should know."

"Well, isn't that something?" Hannah gave a tiny laugh. "I've had a crush on him since volleyball camp. Do you remember?"

"Camp? Of course." They'd both dreamed of playing professionally one day. "I don't remember him, though."

"He was on the boys' side of the lake, but that last night, when we all got together for the cookout? The first time I laid eyes on him, I was head over heels."

"You never told me that."

"I didn't figure I'd ever see him again. We texted a few times, but he had a girlfriend, and I figured any relationship was out of the question."

"And now he's your bodyguard?"

They shared a smile. "In a rare moment, he once told me that it was a dream come true. I thought he was being sarcastic."

Maybe there would be a happy ending to this after all. "What about Chad?"

Hannah gave her a perplexed look. "What about him?"

"You seemed infatuated with him."

Hannah adjusted the wrist wrap, wincing slightly. "Who in their right mind wouldn't crush on him, at least a little? He's drop dead gorgeous and loaded, but trust me, I act that way with all potential donors. The more excited and invested I am in them, the more likely they'll open their purses."

"How did you meet him?" Rory asked.

"He contacted my office a few weeks ago when he heard about the event. Binni told him about it—guess they're childhood friends."

"Oh!" Amelia retrieved her phone. "Speaking of. This boy in the group shot." She showed Hannah the picture. "Do you know who he is? Why don't you two have a stuffed Bluebird?"

Hannah squinted and Amelia enlarged the photo. The First Daughter turned sad. "That's Stanton. We both had those toys, and then some jerk took them. Said he'd give them back to us later but he never did. That poor kid. He was abducted a few days after the event. I remember my parents freaking out, and while they put on a brave face around me, I overheard their conversations about it. They were convinced it could've been me."

"They marked you," Rory said. "By taking the birds, that guy put a target on you for his crew. Do you remember what he looked like?"

"His *crew*?"

"We've been investigating a child abduction ring and believe they were active in the area at that time."

She shook her head. "That's horrible. The FBI tried to get me to pick him out from some photos, but there were so many people there that night, and I was tired and had a stomach bug." She stared at the photo again. "Stanton was kind to me. Brought me some ginger ale. The grownups all blurred together." She sighed. "For years afterwards, I lived with guilt that they took him instead of me."

"The FBI had no idea who did it?" Rory asked. "There was no official report."

Binni ended her call and Hannah lowered her voice. "All I remember is that he was never returned to his family. They insisted on keeping the whole thing hushed up. His parents came to see mine, begging them to help, and against the FBI's orders, they paid the ransom, but he wasn't returned. They were devastated."

"That's horrible," Amelia said. "You never mentioned this to me."

"Like I said, I was young, and while I never forgot it, by the time I met you, it was far in the past."

"That bag." Binni pointed at Amelia's purse. Her words were clipped. "You lost it, correct?"

"It's so nice to meet you." Amelia dropped her phone into the outside pocket and extended her hand. "I actually had two. I love this design and the colors are perfect for me. While my attacker stole one, I still have a second."

Without warning, Binni grabbed it from the crutch and began searching it. "You need a new one." She clutched Amelia's to her chest and grabbed a box from the desk. "We will exchange. You take this. Brand new. Much better."

Amelia nearly toppled over when the package was shoved into her stomach, but Rory kept her upright.

Before she could protest, Binni dumped the contents of the purse on the desk, rifling through it and then handing each item back to Amelia one at a time.

Amelia fumbled with the box as Hannah accepted the wallet and travel tissues for her, then three lipsticks. Amelia opened the bag for her to drop them into. "Binni, really, I'd like to keep that one as well. I mean, I appreciate this, but—"

The designer shifted, blocking their view of the desk, even as she continued handing things over. "You take that one. This one is too old. You need new."

Rory went to the desk. "I'll take care of all this."

He scooped up what was left of Amelia's belongings and dumped them into the new purse as she and Hannah looked at the designer in shock.

"I must go." Binni nodded at Hannah, snatching up her hat and purse and heading for the door.

"Yes, of course." Hannah frowned, sending Amelia an apologetic look. "I'll follow you out."

"No." Binni cut her off. "We'll talk tomorrow."

She shut the door behind her.

"That wasn't too weird," Amelia said, staring after her.

"Not like her at all," Hannah added.

"But she took the bait." Rory smiled like it was the best day ever.

"The USB?" Amelia's shock grew. "Are you kidding me?"

He pointed at the new purse. "And your phone."

"Oh my god!" Hannah glanced between them. "This must be a misunderstanding. Binni's not a thief."

"Hey, that guy Chad?" It was Ian on the comms. "I just watched him steal a diamond bracelet off a woman's wrist. She has no idea. I knew there was something up with that creep."

"Slick git," Moe's curse followed.

Rory opened the door and ushered Amelia and Hannah forward. "Our kidnapping ring is in full swing."

"Here?" Hannah squeaked.

"We'll explain later," Amelia told her.

Masden snapped to attention as they crossed into the hall. "You and I need to talk," Hannah told him. "After we figure out what Binni is up to. What everyone is up to."

"We've got a situation out front," Tate said and Amelia's stomach, already flopping like a fish out of water, went crazy.

"Handle it," Rory demanded. "We've got our own back here."

"One of the kids has been marked," Vivi told him. "Just like Hannah mentioned. I saw a nondescript man hand him, get this, a stuffed Bluebird. Parker? Moe?"

"We've got eyes on him," Parker responded.

"Do not engage," Cal ordered. "We need them to actually attempt the abduction."

A chorus of confirmations came in reply, both from those inside the event and those out.

"I just slipped a tracker into his pocket," Sabrina said.

Amelia's head spun, a flash headache ricocheting behind her eyes. "You can't let them take him."

"Who are you talking to?" Masden queried Rory.

"My team," he told the agent, then to the others, "You handle the *slick git* and keep that kid safe. I'll handle Binni."

"*We'll* handle her," Amelia corrected, gasping at the pain in her head, but mentally taking a page from Rory's book and telling it to fuck off. She had things to do.

"Please tell me what is happening," Hannah demanded.

As Rory led them to the exit across from the garage, she did her best to explain what was going down to Hannah and Masden.

TWENTY-TWO

"You should have stayed put," Rory growled.

Amelia bared her teeth and mimicked his voice, even as she hurried to keep up with him. "You should stop being a jerk."

"She's headed for the parking garage," Trace informed them. "There's too many people leaving. I can't take a shot without endangering them."

"No shooting," Beatrice ordered.

"Too late, anyway," he replied. "She's already inside the elevator. Looks like she's headed to the second floor."

"Want me to follow her?" Connor asked.

While Masden had insisted he could help, and Hannah had demanded that she, too, wanted to get to the bottom of this and was coming along, Rory had stopped them. "No go. I can't be responsible for you and Amelia."

"Cohen will keep me safe."

"How dangerous is this gal?" the Secret Service agent asked.

"Dangerous enough."

"I have two more agents here who can help," he told Rory.

"I don't play well with others."

Amelia pinched his arm. "We can use all the assistance we can get. Thank you, Agent Masden."

Rory made a rude sound. "I get that you want me to be nice to everybody, Amelia, but now is not the time for me to invite them into our sandbox."

"You are impossible! I'm going to beat you with my crutch if you keep this up."

Hannah and Masden exchanged a glance. Hannah stood her ground. "If Amelia is going, I am, too. If this is truly the kidnapping ring that took Stanton, I want revenge."

Rory gave Masden a pleading look. "Get her out of here, please."

"If there's one thing I've learned over the past few years," he replied, "it's that I can't tell her what she can and can't do."

"You're her fucking bodyguard."

Hannah lifted her chin and smiled with glee. "You do remember who my dad is, right? Surely, you don't want to get on his bad side by pissing off his daughter."

It was starting to drizzle outside, and the crutch squeaked as Amelia walked as fast as she could. While she was worried for her friend, she was proud of her as well. Hannah had never let her status turn her into a spoiled princess.

"We cannot sneak up on them with you in tow!" Rory

was beside himself. "Please, Ms. Clemson. You're too conspicuous."

Even as he said it, folks leaving the party were noticing them and hailing her. She waved. "Goodnight! Can't talk now. Call me tomorrow!"

"Hurry," Amelia nudged Rory. "We can't let Binni get away."

He helped her into the elevator. "She won't."

Hannah put an arm around Amelia. "We'll look out for each other. You two go after her."

The doors parted on the second floor. The lighting was poor and gave all the vehicles a sick yellow aura. The concrete smelled like standing water mixed with oil and metal.

They emerged slowly, Rory and Masden in front, blocking Amelia and Hannah with outstretched arms. As one, they stopped and listened, and Amelia turned her head, cocking her ear toward the shadowy level. The ceiling was rimmed with red and green lights, showing where empty spaces were available. Most guests had used the valet service, few parking their own vehicles here. There were more green lights then red.

Rory waved them out of the elevator and motioned with his hand for them to stay quiet. Amelia's fingers clenched and unclenched around the handle of her crutch, her ears straining to hear footsteps, a car engine, anything.

Was Trace wrong? Had Binni chosen a different level? Why was she driving her own car?

"What kind of vehicle does she have?" Rory asked. Amelia wasn't sure if he was asking Hannah or the team.

Tate responded. "There's no vehicle registered to her."

At the same time, Hannah said, "She uses a ride service when she's in town."

Amelia's pulse quickened. "Jose's?"

Hannah nodded and Rory took off, moving as fast as Amelia had ever seen.

"Look for a 1994 Toyota Camry, blue, with a ding in the rear right fender."

Masden followed quickly, clicking on a flashlight and running it across the nearest vehicles.

Hannah held onto Amelia, keeping her from trailing after them. "You and I stay here," she insisted.

"What was all of that *if Amelia is going, I am, too* stuff?"

Hannah pinched her lips together. "I feel like you're my only true friend right now, so sue me for wanting to keep you safe. This is all my fault. These two are in *my* program, Amelia. I can't believe either of them is tangled up in a kidnapping ring. They've used me. Even Chad. Why would a billionaire steal jewelry? For sport?"

Amelia squeezed her arm. "I'm sorry about all of this."

"You should have told me your suspicions. I could've made sure my agents were on guard, looking for them."

Amelia tried to explain. "We needed the element of surprise. We weren't sure who we could—"

"Trust?" Hannah asked when she didn't finish, hurt evident on her face.

Amelia bit her lip. "In all honesty, I suspected Masden was behind the attack."

Hannah didn't seem to know what to say, and finally

offered a gentle hug. "I'm sorry, Amelia. I had no idea those pictures would cause you to get hurt."

They continued hanging onto each other as the men walked the rows. "Not your fault."

"I still have copies, so what good would it do for them to steal yours? Is Kenesha in danger? My mother?"

Cal was suddenly speaking to her. "Tell Hannah I've handled that end. Both are safe."

Amelia heaved a mental sigh and relayed the information. Before she could say anything else, she heard Trace state, "She did *not* get off on another floor. Swear to God, Rory. I would have seen her."

"Maybe she walked down," Rory said.

"All exits are covered," Tate replied. "If she leaves that garage, we'll have her."

"Earth to Amelia," Hannah said. "What's going on?"

"Something's not right." Amelia quickly showed her the comm unit. Her foot and leg were screaming with exertion. She'd pay for all of this tomorrow. "She couldn't just disappear."

Behind them, the elevator dinged, startling her. Hannah dragged Amelia to the side, but Amelia caught her foot on the crutch and stumbled. They fell to the ground as the doors opened.

It wasn't Binni. Chad strutted out and pulled up short when he saw them on the ground. "What are you doing here?"

He didn't reach to assist them. Hannah, chuckling casually and wiping at her dress as she got to her feet, stepped in front of Amelia. "I was saying goodbye to my friend."

She reached back, not to help Amelia stand, but motioning her to stay down. Amelia struggled to untangle her good foot, and said under her breath to the others, "We've got company."

"I see him," Rory said. "Move back. Don't engage."

"Where's your limo and chauffer?" Hannah asked. "Surely you didn't drive yourself."

The man rubbed the back of his neck, then shook his head. "I'm looking for a colleague." He glanced over the vehicles in sight. "I must've been mistaken that she was here." He hit the elevator button. "Good night," he said as he stepped inside.

Hannah stepped forward and prevented the doors from closing. "How many people did you steal from tonight?"

Amelia's stomach twisted. "Hannah," she said in warning.

Chad's brows rose, fell. He cursed in Spanish, leaning confidently against the back wall of the elevator. One hand slipped inside his jacket. "What are you talking about?"

The doors started to close once more. Amelia shoved the end of her crutch between them and they bounced back. "You know exactly what she's talking about."

"Do. Not. Engage!" Rory roared in her ear. "Rule Three! I'm coming up behind you."

Several things happened at once. Chad shoved Hannah hard enough to send her sprawling. He booted the crutch out of the way and smacked the button, then stepped forward and stomped on Amelia's injured ankle. *Crack.*

Pain roared through her foot and up her calf. She squeaked, but he was a thief, not her mugger, and she wasn't afraid of him. "You lousy SOB," she yelled, coming to her hands and knees and lunging for him.

The elevator doors banged into her sides, a new wave of agony exploding in her middle.

And then she froze, Rory's yells sounding far away, as Chad drew a gun and aimed it at her.

EVERYTHING inside him went deadly still. It was the feeling he'd always gotten right before he took out a target.

Seeing a gun pointed at Amelia brought it all back—the years of training, the missions, the lessons learned on the ground and in the field as a SEAL. The men he'd lost; those he'd saved.

As always, he'd gone over every possible scenario a dozen times, making sure he knew exactly how to react and execute his plan.

He only had one job in this moment, the tip of a well-honed arrow pointed at the two people in the elevator.

Save Amelia.

This was one scenario he hadn't planned for. His war cry echoed through the garage even as he sprinted toward her prone body keeping the doors from closing and their culprit from getting away.

Hannah was already there, grabbing Amelia by her legs and jerking her out of the elevator. Even as she did, Chad raised the gun and pointed it at her.

"Nooo!" Masden cried, diving for the two women.

Bang bang.

The agent and the First Daughter dropped to the ground, Masden's velocity rolling them over and over.

The doors closed and before Rory could hit the button, the elevator began its descent.

He grabbed up Amelia who stared dumbfounded at her friend and the agent a few feet away. Blood, black in the gloomy interior, was spreading and Rory couldn't tell who'd been shot. "I need an ambulance, right now," he said in his comms. "Hannah and her guard are down."

Confirmation came from Cal.

Beatrice's voice was cold as steel. "Amelia?"

"Fine," she said, even though she was shaking like a leaf.

"Oh, god. *Hannah.*" Amelia fought Rory's hold, trying to get to her friend.

"Are you all right?" he asked, running his hands over her.

"Don't worry about me! Take care of her!"

"Amelia." He used his no-nonsense tone, keeping his own panic at bay. She seemed okay, but it had been close. *Too* close. She could be dead right now. "Are you hurt?"

"I can't stand," she said, voice shaking. The gleam of tears in her eyes told him she was in pain. Her dress was ruined, stained, torn. "I think he broke my ankle for real."

Fucking. Asshole. Bastard. His list of names went on and on in his head. He removed his coat, setting the folded cane on the ground, and wrapped the garment, warm from his body heat, around her shoulders. The temp was in the seventies but the concrete stayed cooler than outside. He feared she might go into shock. "He could come back. I'm going to place you over here."

She half-sobbed against his chest as he lifted her and moved her next to a short yellow pylon used as a bumper to keep cars from getting too close to the wall or elevator shaft. "Please, Rory," she whispered. "Tell me Hannah's not dead."

"She's not," Masden said on a groan, and they both looked his way. He held a hand against his left side, blood oozing between his fingers. "But I need a...doctor."

Hannah, grabbing her arm sat up and reached for him. Her dress was smeared with blood—hers and his. "Call 911," she ordered them in a frantic voice.

Masden's eyes rolled up in his head and he dropped once more to his back, unconscious.

"Cohen!" Hannah cried. Wild-eyed, she turned to Rory. "Do something!"

He yanked off his tie and pulled his shirt over his head. "Hold this against his side," he told her even as he used the tie as a tourniquet to bind her injured arm.

"Don't you dare die on me," Hannah snarled at the unconscious agent before her. "How dare you jump in front of a bullet for me before you've admitted to my face that you love me?"

A sharp blaring started from across the way. "Someone's tripped the fire alarm," Moe announced in Rory's ear over the noise. "Gonna be chaos."

"The child's outside with our kidnapper," Beatrice said. "It's...wait. Is that *Jose*?"

Amelia pressed a hand to her ear as if she hadn't heard correctly. "He's not in the garage?"

That's when Rory heard a motor rev, the driver

throwing the car into gear. Tires screeched as they backed out of their hiding place and gunned it.

Except they weren't fleeing. Lights bounced on the far wall, then straightened as the car took the corner.

The car was headed right for them.

TWENTY-THREE

Blinded by the headlights, Rory threw his arm up and shoved the First Daughter behind the pylon.

Behind him, he heard the elevator open. The sound of gunfire.

Time slowed, shifted.

He was in the field, performing ghost work for Senator Coleman.

Everything shifted again and he was on a stage, blinded by overhead lights, hearing a female voice—the then-Vice President. *"Ten years ago, we lost a valuable soldier in Afghanistan. A Navy SEAL with over thirty missions under his belt and more commendations in his file than any of you could fathom. He's been hailed by his own men as one of the greatest SEALs to ever defend this country. For years, we didn't know what had happened to him. He was declared Missing in Action. Senior Chief Justin Lugmeyer of SEAL Team Seven discovered Lieutenant Tephra's location in a remote Afghanistan prison on one of his last missions to the area, and with the help of former CIA Operations director, Jonathan Brockmann, we brought him home."*

Home. He hadn't been sure then what that meant. How it would feel. By then he'd lived so many lies, the VP's version was just another story. Not the truth, but then the truth had never done him much good.

"Rory!" The sound of a familiar voice rattled him. It still wasn't enough to pull him out of the past. He heard the gunshot. Felt his knees go out. Felt them hit the ground. Screaming erupted, glass shattered.

He shattered, frozen in time.

"Rory Tephra!" That lovely female voice was pissed. "Goddammit, get out of the fucking way!"

But he was waking up in the hospital, the meds in the IV warring with the pain raging in his body. At least the upper half. The numbness below his waist made him sick to his stomach. "*You may never walk again,* he heard the doctor say, *but we're making huge strides these days in this area. Surgery...physical therapy...*" He tuned the guy out.

His life was over.

And what did he have to show for it?

Medals, commendations, respect.

They weren't enough. Not nearly enough.

He'd given everything to his country and now he couldn't walk.

He wanted to die.

Something hard whacked him in the shoulders, shocking him into the current moment. On his knees, he grunted and swiveled, swift as a fox. "What the *fuck?*"

Amelia was screaming at him, the sound of a car motor

so close he could barely hear her. Muscle memory clicked into autopilot and he found the strength in his frozen legs to lunge.

Landing on her, he rolled them both over, smacking into the solid concrete wall behind them even as the car hit the pylon square on. His comm went flying.

The motor coughed and died. The driver tried to restart it. Again. He couldn't see Hannah and Masden.

Fuck.

He'd never blanked during a mission. He could have died. Could have let *Amelia* die.

Fuck. Fuck. Fuck. Fuck.

The car door opened and he shifted his body, ready to protect her until his dying breath. The guy probably had a gun, was going to finish them right here.

The headlights glowed, regardless the engine wouldn't start. All he could make out was the outline of a slender figure.

With a hat.

Binni.

"You ruined everything!" she screamed.

He saw her raise her arm. Time once again slowed. "My team has this area surrounded," he blurted without a trace of anxiety in his voice. The itch between his shoulders was a maelstrom of fire. "You won't get away." Shielding Amelia, he pushed to his feet, ignoring the numbness spreading down his legs. *It's only in my mind,* he reminded himself. *I am not paralyzed!*

The woman hauled her arm back and...

Hit him with her purse.

Not a gun.

He almost laughed.

She turned and ran.

Without hesitation, he took off after her, scooping up his cane in one easy motion.

Freedom. That's what it felt like. His legs worked, pumping with adrenaline, power. How long had it been since he'd flown over the ground like this?

His laugh echoed in his chest as he snapped the cane out to its full length with a flick of his wrist. Batman's fabric cape fluttered. "I'm Batman," he murmured and whipped the cane at Binni's ankles.

It hit the mark and she cried out, stumbling. Her hat rolled under a parked van as she belly-flopped to the ground. By the time she got up again, limping, he flung himself at her fleeing figure.

She was half his size and took the brunt of their fall. Her chest hit the concrete, breath whooshing from her lungs in a grunt and her forehead smacking the ground. She made a mewing sound and fell quiet.

In the distance, he heard sirens. Amelia screamed. "Rory!"

"I'm okay," he called. "Your favorite designer isn't."

Binni blinked her eyes, but couldn't seem to focus. She blabbered incoherently. He stood, grabbed the woman's hands, and dragged her unceremoniously back to the car. "Give me Masden's tie," he told Hannah.

With shaking, bloodied fingers, the First Daughter tenderly removed the black fabric from the agent's neck. Tears streaked her makeup. Rory used it to secure Binni's wrists to the steering wheel of the car and Hannah cradled Masden's head in her lap, continuing to press Rory's blood-soaked shirt against his wound. "Is he..." She hiccupped. "Is he going to die?"

"Not on my watch." Rory's legs trembled from his efforts, but he rode the high of the tackle. He had no idea if Masden would live. Being gut shot hurt like hell, but was generally less fatal than a chest or head wound.

"Give me your earbud," he said to Amelia, sinking to his knees next to her. The crushed bumper of the disabled car was far too close.

She did, her hands also shaking. "That was... Let's just say, don't ever scare me like that again."

He popped the comm in his ear and heard an ongoing convo between his team, mostly concerned about him. "I'm here," he said flippantly, interrupting them, "and I'm fine. Where's my backup? Where's that ambulance?"

"Fuck me," Moe said on a heavy breath filled with relief. "I knew you were too bloody ornery to up and die on us."

He stood to manually shove the car back a few feet so he could help Amelia out of her crunched up position against the wall. "Apparently, I owe you lunch, *mate*. Next week work?"

A strained silence filled the air. "Blimey. What the hell for?"

"I'll explain later," he said, bracing his feet on the ground and giving the vehicle a push. His lower back barked, along with his weak knee. He ignored it. "The kid good?"

"He's fine, and we have Jose in custody," Beatrice announced, "but Binni and LeFarre got away."

"I've got Binni," he told them, his pulse skipping when

Amelia, now leaning against the wall of the elevator shaft, smiled at him. Total gratitude and something more was locked in that smile. *Love.* "How'd that bastard get by all of you?"

The elevator dinged. Finally, the medical technicians.

"We lost him," Trace groused. "I've been over every exit of the garage and he never came out."

The doors opened. From inside, Chad, the fucker, grinned at him. Beside Chad was the man with the scar.

"Because he's still here," Rory snarled.

Chad stepped out, a gun aimed at Rory's chest.

TWENTY-FOUR

Amelia had edged up the wall that supported the elevator shaft and was leaning against it when she heard the motors kick in. She gripped her crutch tightly, knowing she was going to need more than that once the doctor saw her ankle.

Rory was a hero. An honest to god hero. He'd saved them all.

And she'd gawked at watching him run across the floor, chasing after Binni, as lethal as a tiger, graceful as a deer.

When the doors opened, she slid around the corner, ready to direct the paramedics to Hannah and Masden. She hadn't expected Chad to step out, gun raised.

Aimed at Rory.

"No!" She swung her crutch.

Boom! The gun echoed in her ear.

Rory fell.

Her scream cut through the night and she swung again, smacking Chad over and over again. "You fucking bastard!" The curses spilled from her lips. "I will kill you!"

And that's when she saw another figure inside the elevator car.

"No." This time her voice came out a whisper, her useless foot screaming in pain as she stumbled. "You."

He was older, wrinkled, but it was him. She'd know that scar anywhere.

Chad was on the ground and he'd dropped the gun.

The scarred man bolted for it.

Amelia slammed her booted heel down on his hand.

He shouted; she did too, as searing pain spiked up her leg. She fell. Chad grabbed her bad leg, twisted it.

Agony. She kicked him in the face with her good foot, hearing the satisfying crunch of his nose as the heel connected.

The scarred man smacked her across the cheek. She grabbed his jacket, held on, pulling him off balance. "You killed my father!"

He grunted, tried to punch her. "You're just like him, you little brat. Sticking your nose where it doesn't belong!"

Then Rory was towering over them, jerking the guy off her. He punched the man in the face and Amelia saw the blood running down his leg.

Scar dropped like a sack of bricks. Rory snatched up the gun. Several of the SFI team came rushing from the stairwell, spreading out over the level.

It ended quickly and Amelia found herself in the back of an ambulance before she could get her wits about her.

The next hours were filled with questions from D.C.

Metro and the FBI, along with a visit to the ER. She caught glimpses of Rory and Hannah, but things got blurry after the doctor pumped her IV full of pain meds. She drifted off to sleep, Vivi and Beatrice at her side, assuring her that Rory's bad knee was even worse now after the bullet meant for his heart had hit it. They praised Amelia for her quick actions, but all she could think of was how her heart had stopped in that moment. Seeing him fall, not knowing if he was dead or alive.

She woke the next morning to find herself in a shadowed room with sunlight peeking through the edge of thin curtains. The sound of monitors beeped softly and she had a roaring headache. Her leg was in a cast and elevated on several stacked pillows. She felt disoriented, her vision blurry.

The rattle of someone snoring startled her, and she glanced over to see Rory in a matching bed, looking as bad as she felt. He, too, had his leg in a cast.

She shifted, throwing back the covers and blinking away her grogginess. The pain in her leg was a distant echo, the overall malaise in her body a dull background symphony. She managed to sit up and shoved the bedside table with a pitcher of water and a vase of flowers on it out of the way. While her mouth was dry as parchment and the bouquet was beautiful, there was only one thing she wanted—and he was in the bed next to hers.

Her leg felt like it weighed a thousand pounds as she heaved it off the mattress and lowered her feet to the floor. Sharp spikes shot up her calf and her hip complained as well, the added weight throwing her off balance.

Holding onto the railing, she waited until the room

stopped spinning and hobbled her way to him, taking her IV pole with her. His breathing was even, the blanket thrown back, just like she'd witnessed in his room. The memory made her breath catch.

She touched his wrist ringed by a hospital ID bracelet. "I almost lost you," she whispered, eyes filling with tears.

"Morning, doc." He cracked an eye open and smiled at her. "Right proper drugs they're giving us, eh?"

His British accent was terrible, but she appreciated the effort and laughed, brushing at a tear that sneaked its way down her cheek. "How do you feel?"

"Like I want you beside me."

"I'm serious," she chastised.

"So am I."

She shook her head in exasperation. "You're impossible, you know that?"

He peeked over the edge at her cast. "Yours is prettier than mine."

She gripped his hand tight. "What a pair we make."

"Come on," he said, sliding over and angling himself onto one side. "You need to get off that ankle."

"You take up the whole bed, you big brute. I can't fit in it."

"Course you can." He gently tugged her down beside him, wrapping an arm around her and pulling her close. Their corresponding casts bumped a bit, their legs tangling in the awful hospital gowns, and they both laughed at their awkward fit, but fit they did.

"Beatrice told me your surgery went well," she informed him. "The kneecap was damaged and split into several pieces due to the bullet, but you're lucky. They inserted a few pins and wires and saved it. You can still walk without a kneecap but your leg will be stronger with it. Once, that is, we get you healed." She was already creating a therapy program for him in her mind.

"And your ankle?"

"Full fracture, I'm afraid. I'll be in this"—she pointed to her cast—"approximately as long as you'll be in yours."

"But you're okay otherwise?"

She stroked his face, the flashbacks of not only the previous evening but the night of her attack had plagued her in and out of sleep. "I'm definitely not cut out to be a SEAL or spy. When I saw Chad shoot you—"

Her voice hiccupped. He brushed her forehead with a kiss. "You were amazing. I wouldn't be here if not for you."

She cradled his face in both hands. "I love you."

He kissed her lips this time. "I don't know why," he said when they broke apart. "Though I'm sure glad you do."

She poked his ribs. "This is where you say, I love you, too, Amelia. More than anything and I want you to—"

The next kiss cut off her words and she laughed into his mouth.

"I didn't have this scripted," he said. "But it's better than anything I could have imagined."

"Scripted? What are you talking about?"

A knock sounded on the door. Beatrice and Vivi peeked their heads in, bringing the delicious smells of coffee and donuts with them. Hannah followed, her arm in a sling. She ordered the agents with her to stay in the hall.

"What are you doing out of bed?" Beatrice scolded

Amelia. "I thought having you in the same room would be enough to appease you."

It should have been, but Amelia needed this closeness. To touch Rory and make sure he was alive and safe. "Couldn't help myself."

"She's exactly where she needs to be," Rory growled, all trace of humor and accent gone.

"Two peas in a pod," Vivi said with a wink at Beatrice.

Hannah leaned over and gave Amelia a light hug. "You know the guardrails can be lowered and we can push the beds together so you don't have to cram yourselves into one."

Rory's arm tightened around her. "Mind your own damn business."

With her good hand, Hannah flipped him off with a laugh. "I wanted to thank both of you. Cohen's going to be fine."

"And how are you?" Amelia asked.

She glanced between her sling and wrapped wrist. "I've been better, but the upside? I get to lord it over Dad. Ha! His daughter took a bullet, not him."

"Masden still going to be part of your team?" Rory asked.

"He's already ordering the other temporary agents around. Can you believe it?" She offered a frustrated sigh. "The bullet missed his major organs but did nothing to soften his commandeering attitude."

"Sounds like someone else I know," Vivi muttered on a cough.

Rory shot her a glare.

"Anyway," Hannah went on. "I'll let you get back to whatever you were..." Her eyes scanned their intertwined bodies. "Double date when Cohen is on his feet?"

Rory groaned and Amelia elbowed him. "I would love that!"

They said their goodbyes to her and between all four of them, they managed to get Rory and Amelia sitting up with coffee and donuts. "What did you find out?" Rory quizzed Beatrice.

"The man with the scar is Jan Meidros. He was part of the original international ring, and was supposed to be lying low here in America after the Concordia incident. Instead, he put together his own group and was indeed trying to kidnap Hannah the night of that birding event. I believe, thanks to Baron Thorpe, he aborted that plan, but still went after Stanton. Antoni and Rena decided to keep Stanton, and they raised him to be one of their co-conspirators. He grew up to be known as Chad LeFarre, one of his many aliases through the years."

Amelia swallowed a bite of doughnut. Nothing had ever tasted better. "But I thought he was a tech billionaire."

"The group reunited in Serbia a few years ago, according to what Interpol has already gotten out of him. Stanton, a.k.a. Chad, was good at stealing a lot of things. Learned it from his mentors. Jewelry could be too hot to move immediately after a robbery, but he found he could steal software and digital programs quickly and easily and resell them to the highest bidder. He was enrolled at the University of Belgrade and there came into contact with plenty of students working on various apps and software that he pilfered."

"Again, how awful," Amelia said. "He made all that money off other peoples' hard work?"

Beatrice nodded and sipped her drink. "He and Binni connected through Hannah's leadership group, and the original ringleader, Antoni, saw the opportunity to exploit those funding the scholarships and investments as well as those receiving them."

Rory wiped his hands on a napkin and downed some coffee. "How did Meidros find out about the pictures?"

"Kenesha Wallace," Amelia said.

Beatrice nodded. "She's the one who told us most of the story after Hannah pointed the FBI at her regarding the pictures. Apparently, she posted on her social media about the job with the First Lady and the scrapbook she'd put together about the sanctuary fundraiser. Chad had set up a software program to flag any mentions of that night and his kidnapping, so when the team saw it, they devised a plan to destroy the photos. Chad and Meidros returned here to get their hands on that digital scrapbook and wipe it. They never expected Hannah to give you a copy."

"And Binni? What was her role?"

Vivi set her empty cup aside and fished in the box to pull out another cream-filled treat. "While she actually does avoid being in public, she still did spring and fall runway shows and met with very rich clients to give them first dibs on her one-of-a-kind collections. That got her in the door of quite a few folks around the globe, and she needed her translator, aka Petrina Yokovich, to accompany her. They were smart enough not to steal from every client, but they didn't have to. Petrina scoped out the mansions, the security, and located safes, and then the team would decide who offered the biggest payout—whether it was jewelry, art, or kidnapping for ransom."

"It's a huge bust for us as well as Interpol." Beatrice smiled. "Two generations of a criminal enterprise who are responsible for billions of dollars of thievery, as well as the toll on numerous families."

Including Moe's.

"Why didn't Stanton run away and turn them in when he was old enough?" Amelia asked.

Vivi licked icing off a finger. "Ever heard of Stockholm Syndrome? This appears to be a classic case. He bonded with his kidnappers who brainwashed him to view his parents, the police, and authority figures in a negative way."

For a long moment, no one said anything, all of them lost in their thoughts.

"Hannah didn't recognize him." Amelia wished she hadn't drank the coffee. "I'm surprised she's not blaming herself in some way over that."

Vivi nodded. "She is, but we discussed it. She was only eight and Stanton's looks changed. He fooled a lot of people, not just her."

"Well." Rory wadded up his napkin and shoved it inside his empty cup. "How soon can you bust us out of here? I've got work to do."

Amelia smacked his arm. "Don't be ridiculous. You nearly died and you're on bed rest."

"I didn't even come close to dying." He gave her a squeeze. "And I don't do bed rest. Not anymore."

Amelia looked at the others for backup, but Vivi shrugged. "He's right. There's way too much to handle back at SFI. We can't have him slacking off here."

Then she got it—Rory needed to get out of here pronto. His work entailed therapy about the past and what had happened to him and all of this and what it had triggered. If he stayed in this bed feeling helpless, he would only stew about it and he'd end up right back where he'd been when Amelia had met him.

"I've already instructed Jax to get your medical care turned over to him," Beatrice informed him. "We'll have you both back at SFI before nightfall."

"Noon," he countered. "You've got until noon or Amelia and I are making a break for it on our own."

Beatrice cocked a brow, pointedly glancing at their mutual casts. "You always push the boundaries, don't you?"

He grinned. "One of my specialties."

She stood and began cleaning their breakfast trappings. "I'll see what I can do. We aren't moving headquarters to the new site until next month, so you'll have time to work on that around your combined recoveries."

"*Next month?*" Rory growled. "That screws up my entire schedule."

The door opened and Moe sauntered in. "Look there. The old codger lives. Already giving Beatrice hell, are you?"

Parker entered behind him. "You two look cozy."

"Yes, next month," Beatrice went on. "No arguments."

As she and Vivi headed for the door, Vivi turned back to them. "And you both have appointments to see me tomorrow at three. Don't be late."

"Fuck," Rory said and everyone laughed.

TWENTY-FIVE

Couples counseling was a test of Vivi's patience.

She eyed Rory and Amelia as they squared off across from her. Rory refused a wheelchair, using crutches to get around like Amelia, so she'd pointed her visitor chairs at each other, using a coffee table between them to elevate their legs.

"He's working too much," Amelia snapped, glaring at Rory.

"Look who's talking," he remarked.

Vivi cleared her throat. "This session is to discuss your emotions in the aftermath of what happened. Each of you has experienced a significant trauma—"

"Save it, Doc." Rory rubbed his beard. "Amelia and I are good."

"*Rory.*" Amelia's voice was frustrated, chastising. "We scripted this, remember?"

Vivi eyed him. "You scripted a session with me?"

A cunning grin. "Been doing it all along. You're finally catching on."

She didn't like the look in his eyes. "Doing what exactly?"

"Giving you something to look forward to. You really think I'm that screwed up? Admit it, you love arguing with me, riling me up, threatening me. Gets your blood pumping. You'd be bored silly if I didn't make your life more challenging."

Was he suggesting he'd purposely tricked her into believing he was more damaged than he was? *No. This is his shield. He's covering for his true feelings.*

Wasn't he?

"By all means," she said, noticing how her blood *was* pumping at his provocation. "Fill me in about your brilliance."

She and Amelia both gave him smiles.

"You're smarter than I am, and even you know I don't need therapy anymore, Montgomery. My anger is gone."

"Is that so?"

"Yeah." He tapped the bottom of Amelia's foot with his. "Thanks to her. I've known it for a while now, and so have you. I was grasping at the old Rory, acting like him. Shutting down my emotions, except the anger. That was my defense, my security, to keep you all at arm's length. I don't need it anymore."

Vivi nearly choked. *What do you know? The patient has healed himself.*

"Therefore, the reason we're actually here," he went on, "is because you think I can help Amelia."

The smartass wasn't wrong. She gave him mental props. "In what way, Rory?"

"Trauma is trauma. She and I could have undergone the same exact situation and still processed it differently. Sharing our reactions to it, however, can lead to bonding and a deeper sense of identity, knowing someone understands. It can also help us work through our emotions and find a level of peace we can't on our own. In a nutshell, you want me to be her support group."

Amelia made a surprised sound, staring at him with disbelief.

Vivi nodded. "And how does *that* make you feel, Mr. Expert?"

He grinned. "Empowered. I lived through hell and came back from it. Now I can help her sort through her experiences."

Amelia turned wide eyes to her. "Is that true?"

She raised her hands in a surrender gesture. "You found me out. Please"—she motioned for him to go on—"continue. I think it would be effective for Amelia to hear about an experience when you were a SEAL, or perhaps one of your ghost missions."

"You don't want him to talk about when he was shot?" she asked.

"No. I want him to talk about what it feels like to be a hero, and I want you to listen closely. That's our endgame, in case you haven't guessed, Batman. I want you both to feel like the heroes you are."

Rory settled in, seemingly eager to comply for once. "She's right, Amelia. You had no training and yet you solved your dad's murder and busted up an international kidnapping and theft ring."

"Me?" She snorted. "I popped a guy with a crutch. You went all Jason Bourne and took out half of them all by yourself."

"You didn't let the attack in the alley stop you from getting to the truth. Takes a brave person to face their fears like that," he countered.

"And you went to an event that triggered your PTSD and still managed to stand up to yours."

"Show me your scars and I'll show you mine," Rory egged her on.

Amelia narrowed her eyes. "Challenge accepted, but I get to hear the story behind each and every one of yours."

Vivi grinned to herself. These two were so good for each other.

"No can do. Most of them are classified," Rory said.

"Bullshit." Amelia peeked at Vivi for confirmation, or maybe her look was a plea for backup. Hard to tell. Could be both. "You're afraid to tell me the truth about your past." She reached forward and placed a hand on his raised foot. "I can handle it. I won't judge you. Ever."

He caved at the sincerity on her face, leaning forward to meet her across the expanse. One of his much larger hands landed on top of hers. "I know you won't."

"But...?"

A heavy sigh left his lips. "I've never spoken of my ghost work. To anybody."

Vivi was shocked. She hated to interrupt them but had to know, "Not even an Agency therapist?"

A shake of his head. "I gave reports and even those were...brief. The bosses gave me assignments and all they wanted was confirmation the mission was done. No details."

The amount of shit he carried staggered her imagination. "If you ever *do* want to talk about them—"

"Thanks, Doc. I appreciate the offer. I do, but"—he squeezed Amelia's hand—"if I decide to, we've got it covered."

Maybe he *would* open up to her, tell her about the missions behind his scars.

Amelia pushed out of her chair onto her feet. Vivi tensed and started to warn her not to hurt herself, but Rory steadied her. "You're damn right you've got it covered. Your secrets are safe with me. I love you, Rory Tephra."

He gently tugged her down to sit in his lap. "I love you, Amelia Thorpe." She tucked her head onto his shoulder and the two of them fell silent, lost in each other.

Vivi thought of a hundred things to say, to keep their communication open and their therapy session going, but none of her words, nor their admissions, could do what a simple, quiet understanding could. The touch of another human being who'd survived a trial along with you. The knowingness that came from connecting with somebody who loved you deeply.

And then, of course, they had to go and make it awkward, whispering to each other, back and forth, back and forth, her only catching a word here and there. Rory's husky chuckle let her know what was on their minds right before he kissed Amelia.

Annnnd...this session is over. She made a note on her

tablet and fiddled with a few things on her desk, waiting for the kiss to end.

It didn't. If anything, it became more ardent, more passionate.

Yep, reality TV had nothing on these two.

Alrighty then. She stood, straightening files and removing her reading glasses. "I need to, um, yeah."

Rory's hands were rubbing Amelia's back and she wrapped an arm around his neck, her other disappearing below his waist.

It's like I'm not even here! "I'll just leave you to it, then," Vivi said, clearing her throat and averting her eyes. She headed for the door, wondering if Ian was available for some midday fun. "Lock up when you're done."

As she closed the door behind her, she heard Amelia laugh, light and airy, and Rory tell her she had too many clothes on.

At the elevator, she pulled out her phone and sent a message. *How soon can you get to the library?*

Ian, ever up for a rendezvous, responded with a winky face. *I'm already there.*

She laughed as she pushed the button and then sighed as she realized the two people in her office had faced their demons together and finally found their happily-ever-after.

Now, *that* was romantic.

Can't get enough spies? *Covert Lies, SEALs of Shadow Force: Spy Division, Book 6,* releases in 2024, featuring your favorite Brit, Moe, and the woman who holds his heart, Parker. Don't miss their thrilling adventure.

Sign up for Misty's newsletter to see cover reveals, get excerpts and find out about upcoming release dates!

http://eepurl.com/bP19Lr

ROMANTIC SUSPENSE & MYSTERY

Don't want to miss a single release? Sign up for my newsletter today! http://eepurl.com/bP1 9Lr

Are you caught up with my books?

https://mistyevansbooks.com/book-list-2

SEALs of Shadow Force Series

Fatal Truth

Fatal Honor

Fatal Courage

Fatal Love

Fatal Vision

Fatal Thrill

Risk

SEALS of Shadow Force Series: Spy Division

Man Hunt

Man Killer

Man Down

Covert Affairs

Covert Tactics

Covert Lies (2024)

The SCVC Taskforce Series

Deadly Pursuit

Deadly Deception

Deadly Force

Deadly Intent

Deadly Affair, A SCVC Taskforce novella

Deadly Attraction

Deadly Secrets

Deadly Holiday, A SCVC Taskforce novella

Deadly Target

Deadly Rescue

Deadly Bounty

Deadly Betrayal

Deadly Threat

The Super Agent Series

Operation Sheba

Operation Paris

Operation Proof of Life

Operation Lost Princess

Operation Ambush

Operation Christmas Contraband

Operation Sleeping With the Enemy

The Justice Team Series (with Adrienne Giordano)

Stealing Justice

Cheating Justice

Holiday Justice

Exposing Justice

Undercover Justice

Protecting Justice

Missing Justice

Defending Justice

SCHOCK SISTERS MYSTERY SERIES w/Adrienne Giordano

1st Shock

2nd Strike

3rd Tango

The Secret Ingredient Culinary Mystery Series

The Secret Ingredient, A Culinary Romantic Mystery with Bonus Recipes

The Secret Life of Cranberry Sauce, A Secret Ingredient Holiday Novella

Paranormal Urban Fantasy:

The Accidental Reaper Series

Grim & Bare It

Killin' It (short story for newsletter subscribers only)

Reaper's Keepers

In too Reap

The Vampire's Kiss (an exclusive short story available ONLY on Misty's Store. *Intended for mature audiences 17+)*

Grave Girl

<u>The Kali Sweet Series</u>

Revenge Is Sweet, Kali Sweet Urban Fantasy Series, Book 1

Sweet Chaos, Kali Sweet Urban Fantasy Series, Book 2

Sweet Soldier, Kali Sweet Urban Fantasy Series, Book 3

Sweet Curse, Kali Sweet Urban Fantasy Series, Book 4

Paranormal Contemporary Romance:

Witches Anonymous Step 1

Jingle Hells, WA Step 2

Wicked Souls, WA Step 3

Dark Moon Lilith, Witches Anonymous Step 4

Dancing With the Devil, Witches Anonymous Step 5

Devil's Due, Witches Anonymous Step 6

Dirty Deeds, Witches Anonymous Step 7

Wicked Wedding, Witches Anonymous Step 8

Paranormal Romantic Suspense:

Soul Survivor, Moon Water Series, Book 1

Soul Protector, Moon Water Series, Book 2

Cozy Mysteries (writing as Nyx Halliwell):

Sister Witches Of Raven Falls Mystery Series

Sister Witches of Raven Falls Special Collection

Of Potions and Portents

Of Curses and Charms

Of Stars and Spells

Of Spirits and Superstition

Confessions of a Closet Medium Cozy Mystery Series

Confessions of a Closet Medium Special Collection

Pumpkins & Poltergeists

Magic & Mistletoe

Hearts & Haunts

Vows & Vengeance

MEET MISTY

USA TODAY Bestselling Author Misty Evans has published over eighty fiction novels, as well as nonfiction inspirational journals, and writes romantic suspense, urban fantasy, and paranormal romance. Under her pen name, Nyx Halliwell, she also writes cozy mysteries.

When not reading or writing, she enjoys music, movies, and hanging out with her husband, twin sons, and three spoiled puppies. She's a crafter at heart and has far too many projects to finish.

Don't want to miss a single adventure? Visit www.mistyevansbooks.com to become a VIP and find out ALL the news!

Check out her humorous pen name Nyx Halliwell for magical mysteries https://www.nyxhalliwell.com .

LETTER FROM MISTY

Hello Beautiful Reader!

Thank you for reading this story! It is an honor and a privilege to write books for you. I'm an indie author and every fan is important to me. I pour my heart into each story and do my best to bring you an escape from the real world.

I hope you enjoyed this one, and if so, would you mind leaving a review at your favorite retailer? Or share your enjoyment of it with a friend or family member? I'd really appreciate it, and reviews help other readers find books they will love, too.

Readers are the key to my success - not a traditional publishing deal (had four), an agent (had two), or a publicity team (yep, you guessed it, had several of those as well.)

Those of you who read my books and love my characters and worlds, and who then tell others are like the best of friends. I adore you and will keep writing if you keep reading!

If you'd like to learn about my other books, sales, and special promotions, please sign up for my newsletter at **www.mistyevansbooks.com**. You'll get coupons to download starter packs for FREE, whether you love my romantic suspense or my paranormal. I also have a spy quiz, and a book list you can download and print.

Support me directly (no retailer taking their cut), grab special edition box sets, and get new releases before they are out at retailers by visiting my store **https://mistye vansbooks.com/shop**. I have sales and offer NEW RELEASES early! Check it out.

Last but not least, if you enjoy clean, cozy mysteries, visit my pen name **www.nyxhalliwell.com** to see those books.

Thank you and happy reading!

Misty

www.ingramcontent.com/pod-product-compliance
Lightning Source LLC
Chambersburg PA
CBHW061232210726
48293CB00003B/736